FAMILY FIELD DAYS

Jarrod E. Stephens

OAKTARA

WATERFORD, VIRGINIA

Family Field Days

Published in the U.S. by:
OakTara Publishers
P.O. Box 8
Waterford, VA 20197

Visit OakTara at
www.oaktara.com

Cover design by Muses9 Design
Cover image tractor © James P. Stephens

Scripture is taken from the King James Version of the Bible.

ISBN: 978-1-60290-216-9

Family Field Days is a work of fiction. References to real people, events, establishments, organizations, or locales are intended only to provide a sense of authenticity and are used fictitiously. All other characters, incidents, and dialogue are drawn from the author's imagination.

To God,
My Family,
and the
Good Old Family Field Days
Gone By…

Notes from the Author

In the early 1600s, the struggling colony of Jamestown, Virginia, was introduced to a refined form of a plant that was desired in England. The crop was tobacco, and the revenue it generated helped Jamestown thrive. Later, as colonists pressed westward into the Kentucky territory, there were few ways for families to generate much needed income. For generations, people lived in poverty, searching for ways to make ends meet. Tobacco was once again introduced to a new area, and a new era of farming began in Kentucky.

As years passed, the livelihood of many Kentucky families—like the one portrayed in *Family Field Days*—was based largely on burley tobacco revenues. The term *burley tobacco* refers to a primarily air-cured type of tobacco widely grown in Kentucky and surrounding states.

It is my hope that *Family Field Days* will allow the reader to step into the kinder, gentler good ol' days gone by, where you might not have two nickels to rub together, but family, faith, and hard work mean everything.

1

Break-Fast

It was obvious by the frost on the grass that this was going to be an ordinary winter day. The January sun shone brightly on the barren trees in a taunting manner. From the inside of a nice warm home one might think that the orange sunlight would be warming the valley air, but upon crossing the threshold you'd find out the sun was only lending light and not heat. As I stood staring out the window, I noticed a small calf curled up closely to its mother to borrow her warmth.

Behind me bacon and eggs crackled on the stove and my parents talked about the day ahead. The coffee pot chugged away at its rhythmic task: percolating the finest brew one could ever want. With each puff the house smelled more and more like morning. I could hear Dad's chair scoot away from the table as the coffee pot made its last perk.

Coffee to my parents was like oil for an engine, necessary for running. I had tried to drink coffee once—just so I could taste what all the percolation was about. It was hot, strong, and, to my palate, a little weird. Of course, I did this while no one was looking since Dad had always told me, "That stuff will stunt your growth." I believed him, but couldn't help but wonder how my dad could possibly be fully grown with all the coffee he drank each day. If coffee stunted your growth, then my dad would be no bigger than a tobacco seed.

Breakfast had finished cooking, and I heard the shuffle of tired feet coming down the hall. It was the rest of the Merry offspring. The oldest, Gillian, I called Gil. She was nearly as tall as our mom, Erin, and her long dark hair made her resemble photos I had seen of Mom's high school days. Gillian was also born with motherly instincts that were hard to understand...and annoying, to boot.

Then came Hallie, the wonder woman of sorts. Hallie loved a challenge and spent many days watching Dad work on things around the farm. She'd become quite good at fixing things. She resembled Gillian but was a bit taller. Many folks thought they were twins. Hallie hated that.

With eyes half closed and a look that said, "Leave me alone," a third figure lumbered in. It was Orin, my only brother. Morning was the only time of day that he didn't try to look his best. His fire-red hair standing on end made him resemble a mad scientist.

As far as age is concerned, I fell next from the family tree. My name is Sean Merry. Most folks tell me I'm a clone of my father, Arden. Dad and I both have sandy blonde hair, and I comb mine to the right just like Dad.

I know you must be thinking, *That must be all of the kids,* but, I have to tell you, it is not. Several years after I was born, our family was jolted by the grand entrance of not one but *two* new members. Grandma said they were bundles of joy, and I admit I would have joyfully bundled them up and sent them back if I could've. On this particular morning the twins, Starr and Tempest, were running side by side down the hall, then through the kitchen, where they stopped perfectly and slid into their places on the bench around the table. Wild hair must have been the fashion for the morning because they were sporting an Orin-like frizz as well.

All were ready to dig into the smorgasbord of a meal that Mom fixed every Saturday morning, but we knew we had to wait for Dad to ask the blessing on the food. As we all bowed our heads, Dad began to pray, "Dear Heavenly Father..."

At that point I began contemplating my attack on the food that lay before me. If there is any unspoken truth within a large family, it is that you had better know where your arm is going as soon as Dad says, "Amen." If you were not wise enough to ponder such things, you were likely left with the scrapings of what used to be food. Biscuits, gravy, bacon, eggs...where should I go first? I knew the biscuits would go fast, so I readied myself and listened to the remainder of Dad's prayer. "May you keep us safe throughout the day and bless your services tomorrow. In Jesus' name I pray, AMEN."

No other word has ever matched the power of my dad's "AMEN." If you have ever seen the horses jolt out of the gates at Churchill Downs at the sound of the starting bell, then you can imagine the scene at our table. Giving new meaning to the word BREAK-FAST, we jolted toward the dish of our desire.

My knuckles crashed into Orin's as we both dove into the biscuits. Hallie and Gillian were less intensely involved. They were both "watching their weight"—something quite foreign to me. Both watched closely how much the other got from each dish and were sure to get less than the other.

At the same time, Mom bravely reached into the mob to salvage enough for Starr and Tempest. Starr and Tempest only watched. They didn't dare enter the realm of the arms. You may be wondering where Dad was in all of the madness. Well, he had a way of his own. His hands worked like magnets at the table. As he reached, all other hands seemed to be repelled and at the same time the object he desired was drawn to him. No one dared to challenge Dad at the table.

Little was said for the next fifteen minutes. Only the sound of gravy kerplunking onto a plate and the occasional screech of a fork could be heard.

Then Dad broke the silence. "I've been thinking about raising more tobacco this year. Mr. Malone has asked if I wanted to rent his base and raise it as well."

Mr. Malone was our neighbor. He was a World War II veteran and proud of it. He was getting too old to tend to his burley tobacco crop, so he offered it to Dad.

"Everyone hold your applause," Dad said jokingly. "I know it's a lot to take on, but the base is close and our tractor, Ole Red, needs to be replaced."

Burley tobacco had long been a mainstay of most of the farmers in our area and throughout much of Kentucky. The plants were grown in the fields, and then in the late fall farmers would sell the dark brown leaves. Some families relied entirely on the income that the crop generated, while others, like our family, needed the extra income to make ends meet. The burley tobacco crop was simply a part of life.

"If we all do a little more work, it won't be that much of a burden," Gil stated.

"Oh Dad," Hallie began, "you and I can fix the tractor if we really try. There's no need to take on another crop."

Dad laughed, "Hallie, that's real good thinking, but Ole Red needs some major repairs."

Orin chimed in with a mouthful, "Do you think we can buy a big tractor with a cab and air conditioning?"

"You sure don't ask much." Mom chuckled.

I had always believed that Dad knew exactly what we needed, so I gave him my vote of confidence. "Taking on another crop won't be a problem. There are families smaller than ours raising twenty to thirty thousand pounds of burley. My buddy Brooks Melvin and his family are raising thirty thousand pounds, so I know we can take on Mr. Malone's base."

Only Dad and Mom were smiling. Everyone else was staring at me as if I was on fire. Sure, the task of taking on a new crop wouldn't be entirely easy, but Dad knew best.

Not much was said after that, because we were all visualizing the hot summer ahead that we would spend in the tobacco patch with a hoe in hand. "Family field days," as Dad referred to them.

2

Sitterday

After breakfast, we all went our separate ways. Orin and I followed Dad to the barn. Hallie and Gil stayed to help Mom clean up the carnage left at the table. Of course Starr and Tempest stayed inside and did whatever two-year-olds did on a cold Saturday.

Only an hour had passed since I made my first observation of the cold morning from the window. Not much had changed. The frost was still on the grass in the shady parts of the yard, and you could see your breath as you walked along. Orin, thinking no one was watching, walked along as if smoking an invisible cigar and exhaled deeply into the cold air, attempting to make smoke rings. When he caught me staring, he stopped immediately.

When we reached the barn, we entered with awe. Lying there before us was what used to be our tractor, "Ole Red." Poor Red was now reduced to several piles of bolts, nuts, and other unidentifiable parts. Dad stood there with his head cocked sideways. We'd wondered what had kept him at the barn late. Now we knew.

"Boys, I knew Red was sick last year, but I never dreamed it to be this bad," he said in disbelief.

You see, Red was a 1972 Massey Ferguson that had performed duties from pushing snow to dragging logs. In fact, Red was a well-known member of our community. Each time someone went in the ditch or needed a tow they would get in touch with Dad and off he'd go to serve his neighbor.

"It looks like the clutch is about shot and carburetor's gaskets are so dry rotted that it is suckin' more air than fuel," Dad said while pointing out each part.

"Can Red be fixed?" I asked with deepest concern.

"Anything can be fixed with the right parts and enough money," Dad quickly replied. "I ordered the parts from Gracie Brothers, and they should be in Monday."

I breathed a sigh of relief that Red would get a second chance at life. It seemed only fair for such a faithful friend.

During this entire conversation, Orin was doing what he did best, sitting. There he was sitting on a bucket again blowing smoke rings into the air. I kicked his foot and nodded toward Dad so that he'd at least look like he was paying attention to what Dad was saying.

"Red can be fixed, but I don't know how long he'll last," Dad stated.

Orin and I both knew that without Red, there would be no tobacco crop and without a tobacco crop, we'd never make it.

Dad knelt down next to the piles of parts as if he were a weary pilgrim paying homage to a shrine. He began to clean each part carefully and get it ready to put back together.

He told Orin and me to go to the other end of the barn and stack the tobacco sticks that were strewn out in the lower shed of the barn. The tobacco sticks were about four feet long and were used to put the stalks of tobacco on so they would dry. Late in the fall, when the tobacco was ready to harvest, it would be strung up on the sticks like popcorn on a string. Then it would be hung in our barn to dry. The sticks were reused year after year. Seemingly, after taking the tobacco off the stick to strip the leaves off last year, we didn't put the sticks back into the stack. So Orin and I picked up each stick to make sure it was not broken and then put it in the stack with the sharp points at one end and the dull end at the other. If we found any broken sticks, we tossed them aside to be used as tomato stakes or as tinder for burning.

Now and then we'd pick up a stick and duel one another like two pirates fighting over a long-lost treasure. Orin was two years older and stronger than me, so I was often defeated in this fight to the end.

Dad looked our way. "You won't be actin' fool this summer when you're in the long rows with a gooseneck hoe in your hand. So I guess you might as well get it out of your system."

Despite the cold air, I was drawn in thought to the tobacco fields in July, when the only thing that seemed to grow was the weeds.

"Tobacco hates weeds, I hate weeds, so you kids gotta chop them out," Dad had often told us when we asked why.

I must have really been in lala-land for quite some time because it seemed that only a minute had passed as I picked up the last of the sticks. But as I laid it in the pile, I turned to see Orin sitting again…asleep…on a bucket. I wasn't the only one who noticed. Dad came marching down the entryway of the barn toward Orin with a half-cocked grin. As he approached, he picked up an already broken tobacco stick, reared back, swung the stick, and hit the bucket that Orin was sitting on so hard that it went flying across the shed and Orin hit the ground with a thud.

Orin jumped to his feet, scared and addled, only to find Dad and me bending over and letting out knee-slappin' chuckles.

"Real funny!" Orin exclaimed.

Dad stopped laughing only long enough to say, "I think your calendar must be off a day or two because it's Saturday, and you're actin' like it's Sitterday!"

After a strange silence, all three of us began laughing a laugh that still echoes in the holler.

3

The Valley of Dry Bones

Sundays were special days to the Merry family. It was the only day of the week that we didn't work on the farm. Dad was a firm believer in honoring the Lord's Day and keeping it holy. Of course we never complained.

Unlike other mornings, our house was not filled with the smell of the typical biscuits and gravy breakfast. Instead, Sunday was Pancake Day. Mom would make specialty orders for each of us. I preferred that Mom make my pancakes in the shape of trucks and tractors. Orin liked his in the shape of silver dollars. Starr and Tempest would change their preferences weekly. One week they would ask for puppy shaped pancakes and on others they wanted princess pancakes. I can still picture Mom carefully pouring the batter into the skillet. Her technique was flawless, and she had the talent of a silversmith casting a delicate piece. Gillian and Hallie, along with Mom and Dad, were less particular what their pancakes looked like. It may seem like no big deal to some, but to me a pancake isn't a pancake unless it has personality.

When our craftsmom was finished, we'd all make our way to the table to dig in to our personalized pancakes. On Sundays I could also listen to all of Dad's prayer because I didn't have to worry about what to grab after he said "AMEN."

After we finished eating, we got dressed to go to the morning church service. Orin and I would walk when the weather was nice. You see, we only lived a mile from the church. It gave us the opportunity to escape a ride in the car with our peculiar smelling sisters.

Every service Brother Melvin Force stood outside the doors of the little block church to greet all who came in. He had been the pastor of Shady Meadows Missionary Baptist Church since David killed Goliath. At least that's what Uncle Carve told us. I liked to shake Brother Force's hand slowly because his was so large that my tiny hand seemed to disappear beneath his digits. At the same time he'd look down at me over his horn-rimmed glasses and say, "Good to see you on this fine Lord's Day, Sean Merry."

I'd reply with a simple, "Yes sir" and a smile.

The church smelled like old flowers and old women. As I walked in, my attention was immediately drawn to the many white heads in the building. I didn't realize that God had made so much white hair. I fit right in with all the blondies, but as soon as Orin walked in, he stuck out like a sore thumb because of his fire-red hair. We made our way to our seat near the front, going up and down the roller coaster-like floor. Over the years the floor had been shored up many times by many saints, and the result was a rolling floor that always reminded me of the Hills of Judea.

The rest of the family followed shortly behind us. Starr and Tempest ran in while Gill and Hallie took their time scanning the crowd for any new boy who may be in attendance. Our family took up a whole pew.

At the stroke of 10 our peg-legged song leader, Brother Leroy, made his way to the front to begin the services. Right behind him was the piano player, Sister Paulie Force, Brother Force's wife. She was the smallest adult I had ever seen. As she walked up the aisle she would appear, then disappear, then appear, then disappear as she walked across the roller-coaster floor. When she reached the piano, she would step onto a stool and slide to the middle of the piano bench. She'd lift the lid, cock her head to the side, and await Brother Leroy to call out the page number. On this particular morning we started with number 41, "Bringing in the Sheaves." As Sister Paulie began to beat out the tune, her little legs would swing to the rhythm because they were too short to reach the pedals.

"Bringing in the Sheaves" happened to be one of mine and Orin's favorite songs. During the chorus we'd replace the word *sheaves* with the word *sheets*. I'd look at Orin and he'd look at me and we'd sing, "Bringing in the sheets, Bringing in the sheets, we shall come rejoicing, Bringing in the sheets." What made it so fun was the fact that *sheets* sounds so much like *sheaves* that only Orin and I could tell the difference. I'm sure many people wondered why we smiled while we sang that song.

After Sunday school, Brother Force entered the pulpit and began his sermon. He proclaimed with his thunderous voice, "This morning I'll be bringing a message on The Valley of Dry Bones." He asked that we turn in our Bibles to Ezekiel chapter 37. We all stood as he read the passage. As Brother Force read about how all those dry bones came to life and did the things that a healthy living body could do, I couldn't help but think about Ole Red there in the barn. I could picture Red mysteriously being put back together by a divine hand. His parts, even his worn-out clutch and carburetor were as good as new. After the almighty reassembly, Red could plow a furrow two feet deep and not even overheat.

I was snapped out of my thoughts by a loud "AMEN" that resonated throughout the building.

Brother Force soon wrapped up his message and we were out the doors and on our way home.

As soon as we arrived home, I walked straight to the barn to look at Red. There I stood, thinking again about what Brother Force had preached. And again I could see Red coming together just like new. It was a great thought, but could Ole Red ever be like new or would he always be a heap of dry bolts?

4

Spring Cleaning

Have you ever seen a big fire? I mean a really big fire? Each year one of the highlights on the Merry farm and every other tobacco farmers' homestead was the time of year that we burnt our tobacco beds. We always just referred to it as spring-cleaning.

You see, each year tobacco farmers had to prepare a small area to grow tobacco seedlings. It was called the tobacco bed or a plant bed. Dad had used the same spot year after year because it had some of the richest soil on the farm. He'd marked off two areas one hundred feet long by eight feet wide for the tobacco beds. It was then that we'd commence to cleaning the farm. Every evening for an entire week we'd pick up anything that would or could be burnt and took it to the tobacco bed. Any scrap lumber from the barn, broken fences, old pallets, tree limbs and anything else made out of wood was stacked on top of the area that Dad had marked.

Dad did the stacking. He stacked the wood in a way so that the fire would get plenty of air and burn really hot. The purpose of burning the tobacco bed was to kill any weed seeds in the soil. If you didn't burn a bed, you'd spend all spring trying to keep out all of the weeds that smother out the tobacco plants. The burning also helped loosen the soil up so the little tobacco seeds could come up easier.

During one of our heavy snows in January, an old smokehouse that had been on the farm for ages fell down because of the weight of the snow. Orin and I used hammers and crowbars to pry the boards loose. We saved all of the rusty nails. As we pulled the nails we just pitched them into an old coffee can we had brought along. We'd use the nails to build things during the summer. Hallie and Gil dragged the boards to Dad, and he placed them on the tobacco bed. Starr and Tempest picked up little bits of wood that broke off the boards and took them to Dad as well. Cleaning was never so much fun. Maybe it was because we were so busy that the work didn't seem like work. Somehow Mom and Dad had ways of getting us all involved in the work. There never was much of a fuss. I guess that's one of the things that made our family so special.

Each evening when we were outside, Mom was inside taking care of the housework. I could always picture Mom shouting a halleluiah chorus as we all went outside, and she could spend some quiet minutes alone.

After a week of evenings, we had finally picked up every scrap of wood off the farm, disassembled the smokehouse, and stacked every other wooden object on the tobacco beds. It was Friday night, and it was time to burn.

We never burned the tobacco beds during the day because it was usually too windy, and you wanted the fire to burn slow and hot. Nighttime was also the best time to burn because you could see the fire better, and there was less of a chance it could get out of hand.

As soon as it got dark, the whole family, including Mom, went out to the tobacco beds to watch them burn and, of course, to roast marshmallows. One of the perks of burning a tobacco bed was that you could roast and eat marshmallows until you got sick. And that's what I usually did.

Dad would get the fire burning in a couple spots, and we'd all sit and watch the scraps that we'd collected go up in smoke. Sometimes a small wind would cause the flames to get really high. Orin and I would run around the tobacco beds making sounds like some Indians on the warpath. The night air and the crackle of the fire made it a special time. Starr and Tempest would just sit on Mom's lap and watch the embers glow. They would squeal and jump each time the fire popped.

When the flames began to get smaller, we all moved closer and began to roast marshmallows. Each of us had our own technique. I liked to put two marshmallows on my stick. I'd put them in the flames and hold them there until till they caught on fire. They'd turn black, and the fire would continue to burn the marshmallows even after I pulled them out of the fire. As soon as they were cooked just right, I would let Starr or Tempest blow the flames out. When they were cool enough to eat, I'd eat them right off the stick. It was a taste unlike any other. If you have ever roasted a marshmallow, you know exactly what I'm talking about. Orin had the most dangerous technique of all. He'd roast his marshmallows much the same way that I did…but he put the flame out differently. Instead of having Starr or Tempest blow out the flame, or anyone for that matter, he'd start swinging his stick side to side. He'd shake the stick so fast that the flaming marshmallow would make a *whoosh, whoosh, whoosh* sound as it brightened the night. On a few occasions the marshmallow had come flying off the stick and launched through the air, like Haley's comet. Dad made Orin stop his technique after he set the creek bank on fire with one of the flaming treats.

Two by two, like Noah loading the Ark, I ate roasted marshmallows until I could eat no more. I ate them until I was miserable. I could no longer run around the fire and instead made myself a place to sit next to Dad.

After the biggest part of the wood had burned away, we would throw any additional wood on the fire that we might have. We'd also take a rake and stoke the flames as each piece of wood burned away. When the fire burnt low we'd sit and talk. Dad would tell us stories about times he'd had as a boy helping his father with the tobacco bed. As the flames shrank lower and lower, we moved closer and closer to the fire. The February air turned from chilly to downright cold. The glowing embers let off an orange light that seemed to make everyone look different. These nights never lasted long enough.

When Mom finally decided it was too cold for Starr and Tempest, she took them inside. Gil and Hallie followed shortly behind. Orin and I stayed with Dad until the last boards were burned away. Only hot coals remained when Dad broke the silence of the cold night air.

"Boys, I'm really going to count on you two a little more this summer. I made the deal with Mr. Malone today about raising his tobacco crop. I didn't know if it'd be worth takin' on, but he made me an offer I couldn't resist. He told me I didn't have to pay any of the lease until the tobacco sold. He said if we had a bad year that he'd adjust the lease fee accordingly. Boys, you can't find a better deal than that. Besides, it's right next door."

Orin and I both just stood staring at the fire as Dad talked. It made us feel like bigshots that Dad was relying so heavily on us.

"We'll do just fine, Dad. After all, Sean and I are getting big enough to take on a man's work," Orin chimed.

I nodded but was a little worried that Orin would get us into a little more than we bargained for.

We stood there well into the night, talking about this and that. Dad mostly talked about the summer that lay ahead. He also talked about how the three Hebrew children, Shadrach, Meshach and Abednego, were thrown into the fiery furnace and how that it was many times hotter than the coals of our tobacco bed fire. He went on to say, "Sometimes life is a lot like that fiery furnace. We get put in the fire and we just gotta keep our faith in God and know He will help us out just like He did old Shadrach, Meshach, and Abednego."

Orin and I both knew he was referring to the fact that money was tight and a lot of things needed to be fixed around the farm. Ole Red needed an overhaul, the house needed a roof, and there were all kinds of other things that needed to be attended to. We didn't think of it as Dad's sole responsibility to fix the woes. We knew it was a family affair. Many family field days lay ahead.

5

Faith the Size of a Tobacco Seed

When I woke the following morning, I smelled like smoke from the tobacco beds and my face and hands were still sticky from all the marshmallows I cooked the night before. We all ate a good breakfast and made our way to the site where we'd burned the tobacco beds. There were a few hot coals still smoking in the cold morning air.

Dad was the first to start raking the ashes. We each had a rake and moved the ashes back and forth in order to remove all of the rocks, clods, and leftover embers. We knew the work we were doing was very important. The entire year depended on the germination of the seeds we intended to sow.

After we had raked over the beds two or three times, Dad said they looked fine. He then went to the barn and got his little rolling spreader box. This little contraption didn't look like much, but its job was mighty important. It sort of resembled a little lawnmower without a motor. There was a little hopper on the top and that was where you put lime, fertilizer, or anything else that needed to be spread evenly. In this case we put a mixture of lime and tobacco seeds. You had to mix the tobacco seeds with something because the seeds were so small that you could never just cast them onto the ground evenly. This was Dad's job.

After he brought the spreader box down he reached into his shirt pocket and pulled out three packages of tobacco seeds. Dad had bought the seeds at Gracie Brothers the same day that he ordered the parts for Ole Red. Each package was no bigger than any other seed pack, but it held enough seeds to plant an acre of tobacco. Dad held one pack up and said, "It's 14L8 for the Merrys again this year."

Dad was a firm believer in planting a plant variety that was tried and true, and 14L8 had proven itself over and over many times before. Dad knelt next to a bucket filled with lime and opened a seed pouch. He held the pouch in one hand and poured some of the seeds into his other. We all stood there starin' at the tiny little seeds that came out of the pouch. They were smaller than any other seed I had ever seen. Even smaller than the mustard seed Jesus spoke of in the Bible.

"How in the world can such a little seed turn into such a big plant?" I asked.

"The good Lord has always been good at makin' a lot from a little," Dad replied. "Just look at what he did with a little clay. He made me and you. Little is much when the Lord is in it." Dad's words always meant so much.

Dad measured the seeds in a teaspoon just to make sure that he put enough in each bed. After he'd measured the seeds, he sprinkled them into the lime and mixed it up real good.

After the lime and seeds were mixed to perfection, he'd begin walking back and forth in the beds, pushing the spreader box and sprinkling a white trail of lime and tobacco seeds behind him. You could see the lime as plain as day but no matter how hard you tried, you could not see any of the tobacco seeds.

After Dad finished spreading the mixture of lime and tobacco seeds, we took a roller that we had made from an old water tank and rolled the soil down firmly. This helped to press the little seeds into the ground just deep enough to germinate. After each bed was sowed and rolled down, we sprinkled on a light layer of straw. Then we had to cover the beds with a canvas covering. The canvas was similar to a large sheet that was very light and transparent. It would protect the seeds and eventually the seedlings that would emerge. We tried to recycle the canvases from year to year because they were expensive to replace. Orin and I went up to the barn to get the canvases. Dad had braided them and hung them in the barn. We took them down and carried them to the tobacco beds.

Hallie and Gil helped us undo the braids. As we began to unroll and unbraid the first canvas, it became evident that there had been some critters in it. Little holes kept getting larger as we unrolled the canvas. When we got to the last little twist in the braid, Hallie and Gil both let out blood-curdling screams and began dancing a dance that would have shamed Elvis. Orin and I peered down to see what was causing all of the commotion. Then we saw it: a bug-eyed field mouse. One of the biggest I'd ever seen.

Orin reached in and grabbed the mouse. "Hey Dad, look at this mouse!" he shouted as he stood holding the mouse by its tail between two of his fingers.

"So that's the varmint responsible for ruining the canvas," Dad dramatically stated. "Well, there's only one way to take care of this. Off with its head!" he shouted.

Gil and Hallie squealed, but Orin and I knew Dad was joking. He was just as softhearted as we were. Orin started to walk toward the creek bank, where he intended to deposit the mouse, when the girls once again started dancing and squealing.

"What on earth are you two squealin' about?" Dad asked.

They pointed again at the canvas. We all peered down at the site. There, where the big, bug-eyed mouse had been, were three little pink baby mice.

"Whoa! Would you look at that!" I exclaimed.

Orin came running back to see what all the commotion was about. He saw the mice and scooped them up in his hand.

"Orin, what did you do with that big mouse?" Gil asked.

"I put her in the weeds by the creek," he replied.

"Oh no! What are we going to do with these babies? They're naked and their eyes aren't even open," Hallie lamented.

Due to all of the shouting, Mom and the twins came out of the house to see what we had found. When the twins saw the mice, it was instant adoption. They petted the little mice in Orin's hand and laughed because they had never seen such tiny and hairless creatures.

"Awww," Starr said.

Tempest quickly followed with, "Can we keep 'em?"

There was no argument. The offspring of the varmint responsible for destroying our canvas were swept out of Orin's hand and taken into the house. Mom carried the three blind mice, and the twins followed behind her.

Dad, Orin, Gil, Hallie, and I all stood looking at the holes in the canvas. We covered one of the plant beds with the other canvas. Later, Dad borrowed a canvas from Mr. Malone to cover the other plant bed.

When we all went in for supper, Starr and Tempest were leaning over a little shoebox where they had taken some toilet paper and made a little nest for their newfound friends. They had been using a little baby medicine dropper to feed them milk. Little seeds of love that Mom and Dad had planted germinated often in our family. This may seem like no big matter to some folks, but we each knew that just like the seeds we planted that day, "Little is much when the Lord is in it." This was just the beginning of the harvest.

From that day on it was not uncommon to find an old shoebox with a baby rabbit, mouse, frog, or any other creature that may have been orphaned on the farm. Although their success rate was not all that great, Starr and Tempest both spent a lot of time thereafter taking care of God's little creations.

6

Miss Fish

Sunday came and went in a flash. It felt like Brother Force had barely stopped preaching in the afternoon service, and Mom was waking us to catch the school bus. We all had our unique ways of waking up and, for Orin, Mom had her own unique way to wake a sound sleeper.

Her first attempt to stir us wasn't too bad. It usually consisted of a soft, "It's time to get up." You see, she'd speak softly so she wouldn't wake Starr and Tempest. If her first attempt was a failure, then she'd resort to pulling all the covers off your bed. This particular tactic proved most effective on cold winter mornings. In all reality, I can only remember Mom resorting to step three on one particular occasion.

One rather warm late summer night Orin and some older boys had stayed out frog giggin'. Mom could tell by the telltale signs of wet, muddy clothes and a bowl full of newly skinned frog legs in the fridge that waking Orin was going to be a chore. She followed steps one and two but to no avail. Finally, at her wits' end, she did what Orin hated the most. Mom would forewarn all who were already awake, then she'd go into Orin's room, clear her throat, and let out the most blood-curdling, ear-piercin', wake-up-the-dead scream you could ever imagine. When she'd start screaming, we would burst out into early morning laughter. Mom always had her ways.

After all the morning commotion in the bathrooms and eating breakfast, Gillian, Hallie, Orin, and I would make our way to the bus stop. It was only at the end of the driveway, but at 6:30 in the morning, it felt like a journey.

You could hear the bus long before you could see it. Number 41, which if you remember was also the page number to mine and Orin's favorite hymn, would come roaring down the gravel road and come to a screeching halt, barely missing our mailbox. For a few seconds after the bus stopped, a cloud of dust that had been chasing the bus for quite some time would race to meet you. As the door squeaked open, a new world appeared before you. A stinky world. It did not matter how clean number 41 was, it just stunk. Our driver, Loretti, who also went to church with us, took up more than her fair share of the bus but said very little to us due to fear that she may miss something in her rearview mirror. She'd acknowledge us with a head nod, and we'd race to find a seat because we knew Loretti had no mercy on the bus' clutch. She'd pop the clutch at about half throttle, and we'd be jolted off to school.

Not long after the journey began, it ended. You see we only lived about four miles from Roy G. Biv Elementary School where Orin and I went. Gillian and Hallie had to be jolted another twenty-five miles to the county high school.

Orin was an eighth grader, so these would be his last few weeks at Roy G. Biv. I was in the sixth grade and let me tell you, it was a year of mixed emotions.

Earlier in the year my teacher, Mrs. Barrel, had to leave because she had a baby. I was glad whenever she left because every time she would go down the aisle to check someone's work, she'd either step on your toes or clear your desk with her rump. She was replaced by Miss Bass or "Miss Fish."

Miss Bass was a lady who definitely took things too seriously. She always said she had a sense of humor, but to this day it has not been spotted. Did I mention the fact that her mouth, when opened completely, could block the entire Midwestern United States on her pull-down U.S. map? I also need to mention the fact that she talked entirely too much. She'd be teaching a lesson and when it came time to ask somebody a question, she'd sometimes blurt out the answers before anyone had time to answer.

The whole "Miss Fish" thing began one day in science class. Miss Bass was teaching us the basic anatomy of the fish. She showed us pictures of some of the prettiest salt-water fish I'd ever seen and read us a story from *National Geographic* about an underwater investigation to save the fish. Then it happened.

Miss Bass turned on her handy dandy overhead projector and began showing us transparent images of local fish that we were more familiar with. She showed us catfish, bluegill, crappie, and then, last but not least, she showed us...well, let me put it back into her words.

"Children, now I am going to show you a picture of a Big Mouth Bass."

With that the entire class burst out in laughter. I know everybody was thinking the same thing I was. Miss Bass stood awestruck and silent, not realizing for a minute what she'd said. Then it hit her. We had all talked about how, since day one, Miss Bass had talked nonstop. Once again, her supposed sense of humor was absent.

A look that said, "Enough," began to cross her face. The madder she got the more, she resembled the Big Mouth Bass projected onto the screen. At that moment, the legendary Miss Fish was born.

Although no one dared call her "Miss Fish" to her face, that's how we referred to her when we talked about her on the playground or anywhere else she came up in conversation.

By the end of the school day, the Miss Fish incident had spread from kindergarten clear through to the eighth grade. In fact, it was the first thing Orin asked me about when I got on the bus that evening.

"Who came up with it? What started it? What did she think?" Orin asked in a flash.

I turned to him and told him about the whole thing. Orin sat all big-eyed listening to my story. When I told him about her Big Mouth Bass statement, he commenced to knee-slappin' laughter.

Before we got off the bus, Orin promised he'd never tell Mom or Dad about the incident. Those were things you didn't want to get out because in a community the size of Shady Meadows, your parents may just get acquainted with your teacher and invite them to dinner or something like that.

Stranger things had happened.

7

The Resurrection Morning

Time passed unusually quickly at Roy G. Biv Elementary that spring. Because of the "Miss Fish" incident, the cooks were careful not to serve fish for the remainder of the year.

As the ground began to thaw and the Easter lilies began to appear in the fence rows, my mind was drawn further and further from the classroom and closer to the tobacco fields. You see, there is an unusual stir that a farmer and his family get once the ground begins to thaw. As sure as the lilies begin to bloom, so does the work of the tobacco farmer.

We worked hard that Saturday before Easter. Because of an unusual cold spell, Orin and I spent the morning splitting firewood and stacking it neatly beside the back door of the house. Stacking firewood was one of the things Orin could do neatly. He took pride in his stacks. He would always place the larger logs, what we called "night logs," because they would last all night, on the bottom so they formed a solid base. Then he'd stack the rest with great care until it formed a nice pyramid shape. Like a pharaoh approving a fine pyramid, he'd stand back and admire his stack.

As we split and stacked the wood, we could hear Dad at the barn working on something. We didn't investigate because we had plenty to do at the house and if we went up to the barn, Dad might add something else to our "To Do" list. We'd hear an occasional thump, ping, or rattle. Soon we found out what all the commotion was about.

It started with the small noise of what sounded like our Beagle Smif with his head down a rabbit hole trying to run out a cottontail.

Smif was the fattest Beagle you ever saw, and when he barked, he sounded like, "ROOR-ROOR-ROOR-ROOF." A similar sound was now coming from the barn. Orin and I both looked at each other because Smif was lying at the end of one of Orin's woodpiles fast asleep on an old pair of Dad's coveralls. As our eyes fell upon the barn we both began to smile because we knew that only one other thing on earth made that sound, and it was Ole Red. Our thoughts were verified by the puffs of white smoke that began coming through the cracks of the barn. The cranking got faster and faster, then finally Ole Red broke into the finest chorus of purring that you ever heard.

"Ole Red's alive," Orin yelled.

I dropped my axe and began to run to the barn with Orin right behind me. When we opened the door there was Dad sitting in the seat of Ole Red, and he was grinnin' like a possum. "He is risen, boys," Dad jubilantly shouted. Over and over he said it. "He is risen, He is risen, He is risen!" Dad was a witty man, and Orin and I both knew that Dad wasn't only thinking about Ole Red but also of Jesus' rising from the tomb. All of Dad's shouting brought Mom and the rest of the family running to the barn. Everyone was glad to see Ole Red running because he was our livelihood when it came to farming. We all stood there so long that when Dad did shut the tractor off, we all smelled like fresh exhaust fumes.

Dad spent the rest of the day plowing the garden plot. Just like a brand-new tractor, Ole Red turned over the black soil and barely slipped a wheel. You could tell that Dad was really trying out the new clutch because he was dropping that plow so deep you could hardly see the mowboard.

The very next morning was Easter morning, and fittingly so. Just a day earlier we had witnessed the resurrection of our trusty old farm tractor, and today Brother Force would undoubtedly bring a message on the great resurrection morning where Jesus rose from the dead.

Just as I'd predicted, Brother Force boldly spoke of the resurrection as he shouted the same words my dad had shouted the previous day, "He is risen, He is risen, He is risen." Although Ole Red did stay in the barn more than three days, he did rise. I couldn't help but let my mind go back and see Dad there on Ole Red.

That Sunday was a special Sunday because Brother Force and his wife came over for dinner after church. Brother Force was a big man, and he had an appetite to match.

After the girls helped Mom set the table, we all gathered around the table to eat our Easter feast. Dad asked Brother Force to bless the food, and we all sat quietly as Brother Force began his prayer. He talked to God just like He was sitting right next to him. I even opened my eyes a couple times to see if God was there. It was kind of strange to look at everybody with their eyes closed tight.

Near the end of his prayer, Brother Force asked God to place a special blessing on the farmers in the community. "O God, we know that the season of planting is here for the men and women who tend to this old earth. May You bless them with a year of growth and prosperity."

After he closed his prayer with the anticipated "Amen," we all dug in to the dinner Mom had tirelessly prepared. We talked and laughed over the many stories that Dad and Brother Force told. Dad told us about his three-legged, one-eyed, bobtailed beagle named Friday. Dad always talked about that dog.

"Friday was the most unlucky dog from the day he was born. He was one of thirteen pups that happened to be born on Friday the 13th. That's why we named him Friday. He was the runt, so we paid him a little extra attention. I got attached to him and decided to keep him. It wasn't long until I realized that I had the toughest dog in the holler. It also wasn't long until I realized I had the unluckiest dog. He was still a pup when he took off and found old man Tipton's moonshine still. He must have liked what he found because he didn't come home until late that evening, and we were burning the tobacco bed. Friday staggered toward the fire, without knowing he was highly flammable. He circled it once, and we all sat there as he hiked his leg on the open flame. Like a bomb being detonated, Friday burst into flames. That's how he lost his leg."

At that point everyone was choking and laughing at the same time. We laughed for what seemed to be an eternity. Tempest and Starr just laughed because everyone else was. The whole time I was picturing this poor, smoking, lamed dog running around searching for relief in the form of water to quench the fire. Unfortunately, that is as far as Dad got with his story about Friday. We wouldn't learn the fate of Friday's eye and tail for some time.

After we ate, Brother Force went to his usual resting place, the couch in the living room. He'd prop his head with a pillow and fall asleep. I always thought that might be the time God told Brother Force what to preach on in the evening service. After all, God did talk to a lot of people in their sleep in the Bible. So I was always extra careful not to wake him.

Sunday evening service passed by quickly. Brother Force just so happened to speak on Moses and the burning bush that evening. I couldn't help but wonder if Dad's story about his dog Friday and the whole tobacco bed burning incident had spawned this sermon. Or, perhaps, God had spoken to Brother Force right there in our living room.

8

Long Furrows

For as long as I can remember, we have always had our tractor, Ole Red. But Dad told us about days when he and his brothers had to follow a mule through the field instead of riding along on the tractor.

One time right after he and Mom got married, he borrowed his parents' work mule, Bess, from Papaw Merry. Dad had just bought the farm that we now lived on and wanted to plow the fields for the first time. He brought Bess and a small turning plow down to the field. When he started to hook Bess to the plow he realized he'd forgotten to borrow a lap ring. You see, the lap ring is what connects the horse's gear to the plow. Being young, Dad improvised by taking a bunch of old hay twine and wrapping it around and around the plow, connecting it to the single tree.

Dad put the reins around his back and commenced to plowing. Bess was such a gentle old beast that when she reached the end of the field, you hardly had to give her any commands. She'd just turn and start the other direction. Dad never failed to mention the command words that they used for their mules and workhorses. *Gee* meant to turn to the right, and *Haw* meant to turn to the left. *Gee* and *Haw*... what funny words. I always wondered why they never just said "Right" and "Left."

Dad made a couple of passes, then the plow got hooked on a root from an old tree. Before Dad could get out a "Whoa," the string he used in place of the lap ring snapped and Bess dragged him across the plow slick as a whistle. It sounded really painful, but Dad said that other than a few scratches on his stomach and a few dents in his pride, he was okay. He learned a hard lesson that day.

Now instead of walking behind a beast, Dad sat atop Ole Red. He had mentioned at the breakfast table that he was going to plow some tobacco ground and get it ready to plant. The tobacco seeds we had planted were now little plants and in just a few days they would need to be planted—though we didn't call it planting. Instead we called it "Setting Tobacco."

You'd think that a fella could just dig a hole and plant tobacco and it would do its thing, but that was not true. Tobacco ground needed to be worked up so the plants could thrive. Dad, Orin, and I had spent the previous few days stinking up the whole holler by putting chicken and cow manure on the tobacco field so Dad could plow it under for fertilize.

After Dad greased the coulter and changed the plow point, he set off for the field, promising to let Orin and me take a couple of passes around the field after he got the job started. When Dad reached the end of the field, he dropped the single 16" plow down and began to turn the soil over. There was nothing like seeing fresh soil turned over in the field. Ole Red let out a little extra smoke as Dad lowered the plow a little more. I always followed the plow and watched as the coulter cut the ground and the mowboard turned the soil over. It left a perfect ditch behind the plow that was called a furrow. Dad always made sure that his first few furrows were perfectly straight. To do so he told me that he picked an object such as a tree at the far end of the field that was in line with him and he kept his eyes on it the whole time. By the time he reached the end, he had created a nice long, straight furrow.

I followed the plow because once in a while some buried treasure would be unearthed and I was quick to pounce on it. There was the possibility that a marble, maybe even a stone marble, or an arrowhead, or an old coin would turn up. Sure, that may not be treasure to some, but it was to me.

By the time Dad reached the end for the first time, I had not found anything but a few pieces of broken glass. On the way back down the field a nice cat's eye marble rolled up out of the ground. Not much further down the furrow a fractured stone marble appeared. I followed the plow and pocketed my findings.

About an hour passed before Dad climbed down from Ole Red and said, "Well, boys, I got it started. Let's see if you all can do a man's job."

I was quick to climb on. Dad stood beside me on the running board and coached me along.

Each year he'd say the same thing. "You never want to plow in high range. You always keep in low range. Make sure you drop the lift lever down to the stop bar. Just ease off the clutch and pull back the throttle. If it sounds like Ole Red is strugglin', lift the lever a little or give it more throttle."

I pressed the clutch, put Ole Red in low range, third gear, dropped the lift lever, pulled back the throttle, and let the clutch out oh so easy. With a jolt, we were off. The weathered soil that had been exposed to the winter elements was being turned over and fresh soil began to appear behind me. I always wanted to look back, but knew if I turned around for too long, my furrow would be more crooked than a cat's back. I felt like I was on top of the world, and I was actually on a rebuilt Ferguson. I made about four passes and then it was Orin's turn. Now one would think that since Orin was older he'd know more about plowing and do a better job than me. Well, you see, Orin stayed in his own little world much of the time. Although he listened to the same speech that I did, Dad's message never landed home. Orin placed Ole Red in low range, third gear, like he was supposed to, but he improvised the rest. He had no mercy on the clutch and he let it out real fast. Ole Red jolted like a buckin' bronc and took off down the furrow I had just created. Orin rarely looked forward. He just watched the plows and took an occasional glance in front of him. He went only a short distance and he dropped the plows a little lower. In fact, he lowered them a lot lower. So low that the mowboard disappeared and before he could press the clutch, Ole Red spent out a rut that he could not get out of.

"You buried Ole Red up again!" I shouted at him. Orin had a history of burying the tractor up in the field. At least once a year you could count on him sinking Ole Red to his axels.

As if he had expected Orin to bury the tractor, Dad said nothing. We had to put rocks under the wheels of Ole Red so he could pull himself out. After only a short while, the tractor was free and Orin was back to plowing. Dad let Orin finish the field. After he finished, we made our way back to the house. I walked along the road with my hands in my pockets, feeling the marbles and pieces of flint that I had found in the furrows.

Mom and the girls had been busy making us all a little picnic lunch. They made bologna sandwiches for each of us, except for Starr and Tempest. They demanded peanut butter and jelly. In fact, they ate peanut butter and jelly sandwiches so often that I thought that they were partly made up of peanut butter and jelly. Mom packed up an old quilt and a basket full of food and our whole clan, including Smif, walked up the hill behind the house to have a picnic. I can still remember how the fields looked from way up on the hill. The rich dark soil lay in wait to yield a bumper crop.

When we reached a nice flat area, we sat down to eat. Smif made a few circles and sat down too. After Dad said prayer, we all sat there and ate our sandwiches, washed them down with some ice cold Kool-Aid, and each of us ate an oatmeal cream pie. I've never had a meal that tasted so good.

After we finished, all of us kids started running up and down the cow paths that ran along the hillside. I made the noise of a big rig and Orin made the sound of an airplane. The girls just giggled as they ran. We played for what seemed an eternity, but there was still work that had to be done. Dad was the first to make his way off the hill. He went straight to the barn, fired up Ole Red, and went down the road to plow the fields at Mr. Malone's.

Gil, Hallie, Orin, and I had a grueling task to carry out as well. We had to pull the weeds out of the tobacco beds. It was a tedious job—not to mention it was in the full sunlight. We pulled weeds for the rest of the afternoon and about five o'clock we could hear Dad coming back up the road on Ole Red. He had finished plowing about the same time we finished pulling all of the weeds.

Dad rolled to a stop next to us and gave his nod of approval. In just a few days we would pull the plants from the bed and transplant them into the field. At that very moment a rumble of thunder filled the holler. We all looked up the road and saw dark clouds coming.

"Looks like we finished just in time," Dad said with a smile. In the time that it took Dad to put Ole Red in the barn and we made our way to the house, the first of many raindrops began to tickle the tin roof on the barn.

We were all thankful for a good day's work but unknowing of what lay ahead. That night, as the rain continued to fall, I couldn't help but think that those long furrows I'd walked in earlier would soon become long rows. Long rows that would need to be tended to. With that in my mind I fell asleep.

That night I found a whole box of marbles in the long furrows of my dreams.

9

A Time to Peg

And the windows of the heavens were opened. And the rain was upon the earth forty days and forty nights.

That sure sounded like a Bible story, didn't it? Well, if you ever sat under the preaching of Brother Melvin Force, then you had no choice but to recognize it as the story of the Great Flood. Brother Force had a way of bringing about a sermon that reflected the daily trials of the tobacco farmers in the community. Rain had been pouring from the heavens for a week and then on Sunday Brother Force preached on the Great Flood.

I could not help but wonder while he was preaching if he was trying to tell all of the farmers in the congregation that the recent rain was a judgment from God or if he was trying to encourage the farmers to see past the rainy time to a better tomorrow. I know one thing for sure; we were all hoping for a better tomorrow. The tobacco plants that we had planted in February were now ready to "set" or plant in the field. Every day you could see the plants getting bigger. For the past couple of days Dad would stand at the window on one end of the house and watch the freshly plowed ground turn into a mud pit. At other times he'd be standing looking out the windows in the other end of the house staring at the tobacco plants that needed transplanting so badly. Monday came and went. As did Tuesday, Wednesday, and Thursday.

Thursday evening at the supper table we all discussed the situation.

"So what is the weather supposed to be like tomorrow, Dad?" Gillian asked.

"I haven't really heard for sure, but somebody mentioned down at Gracie Brothers that there was still a chance of rain for the next two or three days," Dad said with his head down.

"Will the plants hold off that long?" I asked.

"I guess we'll just have to wait and see," Dad replied.

"We could trim some of the plants back so they'll hold longer," Orin suggested.

In times that called for desperate measures, we had taken our weedeater and trimmed the tops of the tobacco plants in order to slow down their growth. You didn't cut the plants down too far because you would cut out the bud and if you did that, then the plant was useless. Instead, you were careful just to cut off an inch or so of the leaf tips.

"Yeah we can always do that," Dad said reluctantly.

We all knew that the weedeater was a last resort for Dad.

Dad looked around the table with a serious face and gave another solution for the situation. He looked like a coach of some sort trying to motivate his downtrodden team. "I know this won't be a popular idea, but there is always the option to peg the tobacco instead of using the tobacco setter," Dad said with a look of determination.

His words didn't do much in the way of motivation, but he sure got our attention.

"Peg the tobacco? That would take forever!" Hallie exclaimed.

We had all heard about the horrors of having to peg tobacco. You see, if the soil is too muddy to use the tractor and the mechanical tobacco setter, farmers would sometimes resort to planting each plant individually. To do so you had to first use a string to lay off straight rows. Second, you would use a wooden peg to make the holes. Then you had to put a plant in each hole. Last you would cover the roots of the plant and hope for the best. Pegging the tobacco not only took longer but it was a whole lot harder. Yet, despite its unpopularity, there were times that called for a community-wide pegging party. We were hopeful this would not be one of those times. I couldn't help but wonder if our peg-legged song leader, Brother Leroy, might be a valuable asset to us if we did have to peg our tobacco. He could just walk in a straight line and make a fine row of holes.

"There's no need to complain. The tobacco has to go in the ground one way or another," Mom said in an attempt to give us hope.

After we all left the dinner table that night, Orin and I both lay in our bedroom working on our homework from school. I was busy trying to sculpt a Triceratops dinosaur out of some yellow modeling clay. Miss Bass just finished a whole week of lessons on dinosaurs and had given each of us a small lump of clay. We had to choose our favorite dinosaur and sculpt it to the best of our ability. Most of the boys in the class had chosen to make a T-Rex, but I always thought the Triceratops was the toughest looking dinosaur.

Orin, who was sitting on the other side of the room, seemed to be thinking really hard. He was writing a 4-H speech for his classroom speech contest. One of the perks of being in the upper grades at Roy G. Biv was the fact that you got to compete in contests and maybe go to a competition at the county or state fair. Orin was doing his speech on "How to Build a Safe and Inexpensive Clubhouse." Last summer we had built a new and improved clubhouse, so Orin had plenty of experience on which to base his speech.

For some time all we could hear was the rain on the roof and then total silence. The rain had stopped. In fact, it didn't rain for the rest of the night.

The next day was Friday—the last Friday of the school year. As bus number 41 picked us up there wasn't any fear of a dust cloud engulfing us but instead the fear of being drowned with the splash from one of the many puddles kept us standing far away from the roadside. On rainy days the bus smelled worse than usual. I was more thankful than ever that we lived so close to the school.

When class took up that morning I got my Triceratops out of my book bag. The bumps along the bus route had not been kind to him. One of his horns was missing and legs were smashed into little stubs. As I sat fixing my creation, Miss Bass took roll and the day began as usual. We did Dinosaur Math, Dinosaur Spelling, Dinosaur Science, and we even had a Dinosaur PE that day. Our game was a form of dodge ball, but instead of a person being taken out of the game because they got hit, we would yell, "Extinct." That meant the person had to sit out until the next game. The day flew by, and before I knew it we were back on the bus on our way home.

As we stepped off the bus, the fate of our weekend lay obvious before us. Dad had weedeated the tops off from only one of the tobacco beds. There was also a string line extending from one end of the field to the other. This could only mean one thing. We were going to be pegging tobacco.

Our observations proved to be correct after supper. Gil, Hallie, Orin, Dad, and I spent the rest of the evening pulling plants from the tobacco bed. We were careful to only pull the biggest plants. In doing so we were creating more room for the smaller plants to develop. Each plant pulled up easily because the rain had moistened the soil. Along with each of the plants came a clump of soil that the little roots held on to. We'd place the plants on empty fertilizer bags that made a perfect carrying contraption. Bundle after bundle we pulled the evening away. With all of us working, we were able to pull all of the big plants before it got too dark to see.

The lights did not stay on long in the Merry house that night. We all knew we'd need every bit of energy we could muster when the sun came up.

Just a little after sunrise, we were all awakened by the smell of one of Mom's famous breakfasts. There was no real excitement in the air, but we knew that the sooner we got started, the sooner we'd finish.

After breakfast, the entire family made its way to the field. Even Starr and Tempest could help on a day like today. It didn't take a rocket scientist to figure out how to cover up the roots of a plant. They also provided good entertainment. Everyone had a job to do. Mom and Dad were the official peggers. They dug the holes for the plants. To this day I still think we should have employed the services of Brother Leroy as a pegger. It seemed only right. Hallie and Gil were the droppers, and that left Orin and me to cover the plants. After a few hours Orin and I swapped jobs with Hallie and Gil because it was really tough to stay bent over all that time. Oh yeah, let's not forget Starr and Tempest. Of course Starr and Tempest were so short that they hardly had to bend over in the first place.

To you this may sound like a boring task. It never did register, I admit, as one of the most exciting things we did on the farm. But it was on days like this that we realized the importance of "family" and working together. One plant at a time we pegged that field of tobacco. Each plant that was dropped into the hole and covered made us one plant closer to being finished. More importantly, this day would later be looked upon as yet another family field day.

10

As One Thing Ends, Another Begins

I woke up on Sunday morning with sore fingers and an achy back. I don't know just how many plants we had put in the ground the day before but it sure felt like a million that morning. We had all gone to bed pretty early or, as Dad would call it, "Going to bed with the chickens." Despite the aches and pains, we were all grateful we'd been able to finish at least one field of tobacco. The other plants were ready to plant as well, but nonetheless Sunday was the Lord's Day and the plants had to wait. Dad did not work or have us work on Sunday.

Brother Force's message that day came from Romans Chapter 12 and was about how the Church is the Body of Christ and how each member made up an essential part of that body. He said that some members were fingers, some were ears, and I guess he named almost every other essential body part. "When we all work together, the Lord's work will be accomplished and the Father will be pleased," Brother Force belted.

Throughout the message I was thinking about our day in the field and how each member of the Merry family contributed to the effort yesterday. I don't know if I was a finger, toe, eye, or what I was, but I sure do know that when all of the Merrys work together, the farm work is accomplished and Dad is pleased.

That afternoon was uneventful. We spent most of the time just sitting out back under the shade of the Catalpa tree. The white blooms were falling off the tree, and Gil and Hallie were teaching Starr and Tempest how to make little stick people with Southern Belle dresses using the blooms. Mom and Dad both sat on the porch reading their

Bible. Orin was putting the finishing touches on his 4-H speech. He must have practiced his speech fifty times that day. He really wanted to earn a day out of school to go to the county fair. He had to give his speech on Tuesday, which was the last day of school. I just played with a toy truck in the dirt at the base of the Catalpa tree. Days like this never lasted long enough.

Monday came and went. The only important event of the day was when I had to recite my multiplication tables to the class. From the 1s to the 12s. We each had to recite them. Do you know how terrible it is to sit and listen to 23 students recite their times tables? Well, let me tell you, it was so bad that I started doing some multiplication of my own. I had overheard Dad say that there were 138 tobacco plants in each row that we planted Saturday. When we finished there were 24 rows.

$$\begin{array}{r} 138 \\ \underline{\times\ 24} \end{array}$$

About the time I wrote the problem on my paper, *WHAM!!!* Miss Bass had caught me not paying attention and had smacked the top of my desk. With that, she wadded up my paper and, needless to say, I didn't finish my problem. I was glad to see the day end.

Tuesday was a blur because it was the last day of school until next school year. We spent most of the day cleaning the classroom and packing up our belongings. The last thing Miss Bass did that day was weigh and measure each member of our class. The boys in the class always wanted to go first. We were eager to grow and gain weight. The girls meandered near the end of the line and tried to be last. Miss Bass weighed us on a set of old-fashioned doctor's scales that had been donated to the school. I weighed in at a whopping 96 pounds. I gained 8 pounds that year. To check our height we had to stand up straight with our back to a wall that had an old measuring stick taped to it. Miss Bass would then take a small ruler, place it on our head, and extend it to the other measuring stick. Once in a while a young lad would try to fool Miss Bass by standing on his tiptoes. She'd promptly whack him on the head with a ruler. I backed up to the measuring stick, careful not to even make Miss Bass think I was trying to fudge my height. She placed her ruler on my head and said, "Four feet and ten inches." I was well on my way to being five feet tall.

Not long after she finished measuring and weighing us, the last bell of the day rang and school was out. Finally, summer break had arrived. I left the classroom and didn't look back. The only thing that stood between summer and me was a short ride on stinky number 41.

As we were riding the bus home that day, I thought back on the year gone by to see if I had learned anything. I learned that people who claim to have a sense of humor should show evidence of it. I learned all about dinosaurs and all kinds of other things that I would use later in life. (At least that's what I was told.) Meanwhile, Orin sat on the other side of the aisle clutching a blue ribbon. His speech was perfect, so he said, and he was going to sweep the judges off from their feet this fall at the county fair. He had also been promoted to the high school so his head was extra-large that whole afternoon.

Hallie and Gil had both been promoted as well. Next year Gillian would be in the 12th grade and Hallie would be in the 11th. I was glad they'd both be at the high school to keep an eye on Orin.

As old number 41 rolled to a stop at the end of our driveway, I made sure I was the first one to hit the aisle. As we got off the bus, Loretti gave each of us a small chocolate candy bar. It was her way of being nice to the kids on her bus. (The last day of school each year could have been the only time she was ever nice to us.) I took my candy bar and said, "Thanks, Loretti. See you this summer at church." She waved good-bye and after we each got off, she drove away.

I felt like a weary pilgrim who had been on a journey and finally reached Canaan Land. Summers were priceless in so many ways. Yes, there was a lot of work to do, but there was also a lot of water and sun to soak up. As one thing ends, another begins.

11

Leading by Example

The first couple days of summer break were ours. Dad had been working extra long hours trying to make up for time he'd lost during the rainy spell. He'd leave before daylight and rarely get home before dark. I don't know how he did it. Dad realized that we all needed at least a few days to unwind before we got down to business. And speakin' of business, Friday we got busy.

Although Dad had left early as usual, he made sure we knew what to do before he went to bed the night before.

"The ground down at Mr. Malone's is in good shape, so we'll need to set that field first thing on Saturday," he said before going to roost. "We'll need twice as many plants as we had the other day when we pegged the half acre."

We had always been taught that it took about 8,000 tobacco plants to set an acre. I don't know who took the time to count them, but that was always the number we used. After Dad went to bed, I jotted down the same problem I'd attempted in Miss Bass' class on Monday. Only this time there was no reason to be afraid.

$$\begin{array}{r} 198 \\ \underline{\times\ 24} \\ 4752 \end{array}$$

So we had only planted about a half acre last Saturday. It sure seemed like a lot more.

That night we all turned in early because we knew we had to get an early start. Dad wouldn't be home to help us pull plants, so it was going to take a long time. We knew Mom would be busy watching Starr and Tempest and wouldn't be able to help.

It seemed that my head had just hit the pillow and Mom was at the foot of my bed waking me so we could get started pulling plants. Believe it or not, Orin had gotten out of bed before me and had been outside watering down the tobacco beds. You had to put just enough water on the plant beds to make the soil damp. This made the plants roots easier to pull out of the ground. That way you did as little damage as possible to the plant's roots.

We all ate light because we knew we'd be doing a lot of bending over. As we made our way out to the plant beds we scratched Smif on the head as we walked past him. Every time we went out the door, he was there to greet us. We each went to the barn and grabbed an armload of old fertilizer bags to put the plants on. Smif just followed along.

We started pulling plants from the plant bed that we had weedeated the tops off from last week. Already the plants had grown back to their original height and you could hardly tell they'd been trimmed. It was best to always start at the edge of the plant bed and work your way toward the middle. As you pulled the plants, openings would begin to appear in the plant bed and you could put your feet in the bare spots and reach further toward the middle. Sometimes there were no bare spots that opened up so we'd take a long 2x6 board and span the distance across the bed after laying the board on two concrete blocks. There seemed to always be a way to solve a problem. Sometimes you just had to get practical.

The morning sun began to climb across the sky.

"How many plants do you reckon each one of these bags will hold?" Hallie asked as she completely filled a bag.

"I'd say there are at least 100 or more," Gil replied.

"Why don't you just count a bag and see?" I asked.

"Yeah, that would be a great idea. That way we'd know when we have enough," Orin said excitedly. There wasn't one of us that wanted to pull a plant more than we had to.

So Hallie began counting the plants while the rest of us continued pulling. Each year I was so amazed how that the small plants we pulled were able to survive and grow into the enormous plants they'd become. Some of the plants would be at least 6-7 feet tall when they were mature.

"There are about 150 plants on this bag that I filled," Hallie said as she finished counting.

Gil squatted down to the ground and began to scratch out a division problem, 8,000 divided by 150. After a little bit of figuring, she said, "It's going to take between 53 and 54 bags to set the entire acre."

"We've already pulled 29 bags," I said. "And we haven't even started pulling from the other bed." There were going to be plenty of plants to do our job on Saturday.

Somewhere around noon we took a short break to eat a sandwich and wash it down with some Kool-Aid. We finished pulling the plants early in the afternoon. Just to be on the safe side, we pulled 58 bags of plants. We were going to pull 60 bags, but we ran out of bags. We carried each bag of plants to the shed in the barn so the roots wouldn't dry out too much, and the sun wouldn't make them wilt. They had a long journey ahead of them, so we did what we could to make it easy on the plants.

For the remainder of the day we played around the house and helped Mom pick up around the yard. Starr and Tempest followed us everywhere we went. At one point I was picking up some sticks that had fallen from a tree. Starr and Tempest filled their little arms with twigs and followed me to the edge of the yard, where I dropped the sticks. They did just about everything I did. It was then I realized the importance of being a good example for them.

Dad got home early enough to make sure we had pulled enough plants. I watched as he counted the bags. "Fifty-eight bags. That should be enough," he said after he finished counting. Boy, was I glad to hear that. Then Dad backed the truck up to the shed and we loaded the bags of plants onto the truck so they'd be ready to take to Mr. Malone's in the morning.

That night we had a family devotion...something we did from time to time. I liked it because Dad could sure explain the Scriptures as plain as day. That night he read from the book of Ecclesiastes, chapter 3. He only read the first two verses, but their reality still rings true to this day.

"To every thing there is a season, and a time to every purpose under the sun. A time to be born, and a time to die; a time to plant and a time to pluck up that which is planted," he boldly read. He went on to tell us that we were all going to see the Scriptures fulfilled in the morning. I can still see his face as he explained how we had planted the little seeds, and now we had plucked up the seedlings to be replanted yet again.

"You see, kids, we are actually giving these tobacco plants a second chance at life. If we'd have left those plants in those plant beds they'd never amount to anything because they were too crowded. Tomorrow we're gonna put them back in the ground but not before we apply some water to the roots. That's the way God works in our lives, you see. He takes us from the crowded places that He knows aren't good for us if we trust in His Son Jesus as Savior. That's when the living water is applied to our lives. Then He gives us that second life."

How much more plain can you get? Dad always wanted us to use the Lord's word as a guide, and he led by example.

12

A Time to Set

Mornings in May were particularly beautiful in Shady Meadows. The new blades of grass growing in the pasture gave the hillside a beautiful appearance of softness. The places where the sun shined looked like a green emerald sparkling with little drops of morning dew on them. The chickens were milling about the barnyard scratching the ground and chasing bugs that had ventured out to soak up some sun. Smif was somewhere up the holler, and it sounded like he was on the trail of a rabbit. Long howls were a sign that he was closing in on the cottontail.

"Can't stand around here all day," Dad said as he rubbed my head.

"Yeah, I know. I was just listening to the sound of the morning," I replied.

"Well, what exactly does the morning sound like?" Dad asked.

"Like a lot of things. Like chickens and Smif," I said jokingly.

At the same time I was replying, a big rooster let out a morning crow. "ER-A-ER-A-ERRRRRRRRRRR!!!!!!"

Dad poked me in the arm. "You see, even the rooster knows it's time to get started. MERRYS GET TO WORRRRRRRRRRK!!!" He even flapped his arms to give his battle cry more effect.

We made our way toward the barn where the truck and Ole Red were. Dad fired up Ole Red and took him around the barn to hook the tobacco setter up. *Mechanization*—what a wonderful thing. The tobacco setter was not a high-tech gadget by any means, but it sure did save a feller from peggin' his crops.

The setter had two strange wheels that had a series of chains and rotating arms attached to the chains. As the wheels rolled along the ground, the little arms rotated around toward the people on the setter.

The workers would take turns placing plants into the arms. As the arms lowered toward the ground, the arms closed up on the plants and held them in place until they reached a furrow that was being cut by a shoe. The shoe was a plow of sorts that dragged in the dirt and made the furrow. When the plants were in the furrow, the arms released the plants and they were dropped into the furrow. At the same time, a blast of water would come down a hose from a barrel and give the plant a drink of water, fertilizer, and any other pesticides the farmer chose. The two strange wheels then covered the plants roots. Over and over and over, the process was carried out.

The people who rode on the setter had a tray in front of them. We'd fill each tray with plants to be planted. We'd refill each tray when we reached the end of the row. Most of the time Mom and Gil were the ones who got to ride on the setter. Hallie and Orin did a job we called "Pig tailin.'" This just meant that you followed the setter and put plants where they may have been missed and uncovered plants that were covered by dirt. I spent most of my time carrying bags of plants to everybody. Not to mention, I had to take care of Starr and Tempest. They weren't too bad. They just ate a lot of dirt and played most of the time.

After hooking up the setter, Dad made his way down to the watering hole to fill the barrel with water. Mom drove us down the road in the truck, where we put several bundles of plants at one end of the field before taking the rest to the far end.

I jumped out of the back of the truck and went over to help Dad fill the barrel. Dad used a five-gallon bucket to fill the fifty-five-gallon barrel. Bucket after bucket. It seemed he'd never get it filled. Each time the bucket hit the water little minnows swam against the current, then ended up going into the bucket anyway. What a struggle it must have been.

Finally, the barrel was full. Dad pulled Ole Red out of the creek and to the beginning of the field where we planned to start. There was one more thing he had to do before we could begin. In the barrel, Dad put in some liquid fertilizer and some awful smelly concoction that was supposed to keep away the cutworms that killed the plants. The fertilizer was a green liquid that helped the plants get off to a healthy start. The stink seemed to linger forever. At the same time, Orin and I filled the trays with plants.

Dad climbed up on Ole Red and asked, “Everybody ready?” He knew we were, but he asked anyway. Mom and Gil climbed aboard the setter, just as I had figured. Dad put Ole Red in second gear, low range and started creeping down the field. You had to go really slow when you set tobacco, otherwise your workers could never keep up.

Each plant that Mom and Gil put into the setter would magically appear behind the setter. Proud and green, the little plants stood with the soft dirt around them. The fresh soil was so soft on your feet. It felt good to walk barefoot. You just had to watch out and not step on the occasional shard of glass that would appear in the soil.

Dad sat keen and serious as he made the first row. Just like in plowing, you had to pick a spot off in the distance to focus on and keep your eyes on it. This helped to make your first row nice and straight. After that, you had the tractor tire tracks to follow. Dad was always sure to explain all of this to us.

Plant by plant and row-by-row, we worked throughout the morning hours. About every six rows we had to refill the barrel with water, fertilizer, and that stinky stuff. I made sure that I went to the water hole each time to help fill the barrel. Dad would “accidentally” splash us as we stood watching. The cool water felt good as the day began to warm up. From the field to the watering hole and back was also the only time that Orin and I got to ride on the setter. Dad would let us sit in the seats where Mom and Gil had been as he made his way to get the water.

No time was ever wasted, because we knew Dad had a goal and we had to achieve it. His foresight was always amazing. He planned everything with expert skill so the work would be doable and, come time to sell the crop, payments could be made.

We continued to fill the field with new life. Each person did their job and we talked as we worked. Mom and Gil were carrying on their own “woman” conversation; Hallie, Orin, and I were talking about how long the rows seemed to be; Starr and Tempest sharpened their chompers on dirt clods. Once in a while, Mom or Gil would set a plant upside down so that the roots were pointing upward. They’d laugh as we discovered their folly and have to fix the plant. They said they did this to keep us on our toes.

Dad had once told us of how he and Uncle Carve had taken some old chicken feet that they picked up after killing their fryers and played a similar trick.

They were both setting tobacco on the setter and their sisters were pig tailin'. When the girls were not paying attention, Dad and Uncle Carve put the chickens' feet in the setter arms. Instead of nice healthy plants appearing behind the setter, there were ten chicken feet standing tall in the row. The girls screamed when they discovered what the boys had done. Dad always had great stories.

After setting twenty-four rows, we took a lunch break. Dad shut Ole Red off and we found a shade to sit in while we enjoyed our fine field-side spread. Dad began to pray and at the same time, Smif, who was still chasing cottontails, closed in on one. He rounded Mr. Malone's barn with the rabbit only a few yards ahead of him. Despite his apparent weight problem, Smif sure could run. That crazy rabbit paid no attention to us sitting at the edge of the field and ran through the middle of our picnic. Starr and Tempest squealed while the rest of us howled with laughter. The rabbit passing through our gathering wasn't so bad, but when Smif came through, he brought mud, stink, and slobber with him. There was nothing we could do but laugh. Dad laughed so hard he nearly choked.

Smif stayed on the trail of that rabbit long after we recommenced to setting the remainder of the plants. Dad said we had enough room left in the field to set about eight more rows. It really didn't take too long to set the field that day, but it was all because we each took part. I can't imagine what it would be like for some of our neighbors who had only a few kids to help with the crops. Sometimes I wondered if that was why Mom and Dad had so many kids. Despite my wondering, I knew they had each of us because they had plenty of love to go around.

By the time we finished, the shadows of the trees were stretching far down the field. We picked up all of the fertilizer bags and headed for home. When we arrived, we found that Smif had returned home before us. He lay in his usual spot, snorin' up a storm.

Although the big job of the day was finished, there was still work to be done. Mom took Starr and Tempest in to take a nap and the rest of us helped Dad plant some beans, corn, and all sorts of other things in the garden. Dad always set aside about a quarter acre of good ground to grow some summer veggies. Mom would can anything that we had extra for winter use. The work wasn't grueling, but it sure made us appreciate the food we'd eat later. Like I said earlier, Dad had great foresight.

"If all goes well, by this time next Saturday we'll have all our tobacco set," Dad said optimistically.

"And if all goes well, there'll be a bumper crop of tobacco this year and plenty of fresh food to eat," Hallie said as she raked dirt over three kernels of corn.

"If all goes well," Dad replied. "If all goes well."

13

The Cutworm War

"And the Lord prepared a gourd, and made it to come up over Jonah, that it might be a shadow over his head, to deliver him from his grief. So Jonah was exceeding glad because of the gourd. But God prepared a worm when the morning rose the next day, and it smote the gourd that it withered."

Brother Force began his Sunday morning sermon with those words that came from the book of Jonah. He told us how Jonah had followed the Lord's command and preached to the people of Nineveh, but he still had bitterness in his heart against the Ninevites. I could picture that big old gourd vine sheltering Jonah. I could also picture that pesky old cutworm as he ate away at the stem of the gourd vine. Little did I know that Brother Force's sermon was a foreshadowing of the ordeal we were about to face.

After the service, Orin and I walked home. As we passed Mr. Malone's farm we walked past the field of tobacco we had just set the day before. Most of the plants were wilted and laying almost flat to the ground. This was nothing to worry about because the plants almost always wilted for a day or two after they were replanted because of the shock to their poor little roots. After all, they had been pulled up out of their cozy beds and placed into a strange field. In a few days each of those plants would stand right back up.

As we drew closer to our home, we passed the field of tobacco that we had pegged two weeks ago. That's when we noticed a problem. Much like the field at Mr. Malone's, there were plants in this field that were wilted as well. It wasn't the whole field, nor was it a majority of the plants, but it was still enough to cause alarm.

"Cutworms!" Orin said as he stopped to look at the field.

"Yep. No doubt we have a problem," I replied.

You remember I told you we put some stinky stuff in the water when we set the field of tobacco at Mr. Malone's? Remember what it was for? That's right! It was to keep the cutworms away. When we pegged this field by the house we didn't use water or cutworm stinky stuff. The ground was so wet there was no need to water the plants.

In order to verify that cutworms were the culprits, Orin and I stepped into the first row and knelt down next to a wilted plant. Orin began to excavate the dirt around the stem of the plant. He had no more than broken the surface when he discovered a place in the stem that had been chewed on by a worm. Orin continued to pull the dirt away and then, lo and behold, there squirming in the dirt was a dastardly old cutworm. Orin picked up the worm, and we both looked at the ugly thing.

"I'd stay underground too if I was so ugly," Orin said to the worm.

"What are we gonna have to do?" I asked Orin.

"Well, I guess we'll have to ask Dad," Orin replied. "But I know what we're gonna have to do with this worm." With that Orin held the worm between two fingers and pulled the little guy in half. He threw the worm down and we made our way to the house.

Everyone else had already arrived home.

"Dad!" Orin shouted as we went in. "Did you notice the plants out in the field and how they have wilted?"

"Yeah, I know. We have a bit of a problem," Dad replied.

"What are we going to do?" I asked.

"We're gonna do the only thing we can. We'll have to dig up each wilted plant, find the worm, and plant a new plant," Dad said.

"Eww!! You mean we'll have to touch those nasty little cutworms?" Hallie said in disgust.

"Oh, they're just worms. You'll get over it," Dad replied with a smile.

After dinner, Orin and I spent the rest of the day contemplating what we were gonna have to do tomorrow.

The very next morning, we got up early to wage war against the cutworms. Gil and Hallie went out to the tobacco bed to pull a couple bags of plants to replace the wilted ones. They had delegated Orin and me to dig up the worms. They volunteered to replant. That was fine with me, because I had a plan that would turn our work into fun.

"Orin, I think we need to put these terrible worms on trial for what they have done to our crop," I told him. I had actually thought of the idea the day before, but I knew no trials would be allowed on Sundays.

"I think you're right," Orin said with a nod. "You go get a bucket to collect the worms, and I'll start diggin'."

I set off to get a bucket, only to return with an empty coffee can. By the time I reached Orin, he had a handful of squirming worms. Orin dropped the worms into the can and we both commenced to excavating worms. Every plant was important to the tobacco farmer, so we were careful to dig up each plant that appeared to have the slightest sign of wilt. We had decided we'd have one trial for all of the worms because we knew they had each committed the same crime.

Hallie and Gil were now in the field putting new plants in the holes that Orin and I had created. Row by row we checked for wilted plants. It actually took longer to find the worms than to replant so Hallie and Gil finally caught up to us.

"You guys are so gross. I can't believe you'd touch those nasty worms," Gil said.

"Oh, they're not so bad," Orin joked while holding a cutworm up in Hallie's face. She smacked his hand away.

We continued until we found the last worm and the last wilted plant was replaced. It was now time for the trial of the century: *The Cutworms vs. The Merry Boys.*

Orin was the judge, and I was the prosecuting attorney. The scales of justice were a bit skewed because there was no defense attorney present to defend the worms. Orin sat on a milk crate with the can of worms in front of him as I began my argument. I had seen enough courtroom dramas on T.V. and read about a few in school, so I had a good idea how to act like a real lawyer.

"Ladies and gentlemen, each of these worms are guilty of trying to destroy the tobacco crop of the Merry family," I began. "The crop that these squirmy villains tried to devour is a mainstay for the entire family." I was now pacing back and forth as if I had a jury before me.

"What if these worms and their friends would have succeeded in devouring the whole crop? Well, I'll tell you what would have happened. The Merry kids would have to be placed into an orphanage, because there wouldn't be enough money to buy food for them. Ole Red would never be able to receive the repairs that he needed. I think that should be enough to convince you that these worms are guilty of trying to subject the Merry family to poverty!!" I shouted.

"So what do you think we should do with these worms?" Orin asked with a sincere look.

"I think there is no question that these worms deserve the death penalty!" I answered.

Orin stood up and held the can of worms high above his head. "Ladies and gentlemen, I sentence each of these worms to death by ingestion. Court adjourned."

He led the way to the chicken house, where the sentence would be carried out...immediately.

When the chickens saw us coming with the can, they knew we had something for them to eat. They began cackling and flying around the outside wire pen. Orin held the can above the pen and began to dump the worms. The worms hardly reached the ground before a hungry chicken gobbled them up. One by one the worms were devoured, never to destroy another tobacco plant on the Merry farm. They were each an example to the rest of the worm kingdom that if you did the crime, then you paid the price.

14

Happy Birthday to Two

In spite of all the headaches that Starr and Tempest caused, they were also the cause of much celebration each year on the fourth day of June. Three years had now passed since I awoke to an unusual amount of clamor in the Merry household. I remembered it like it was yesterday.

I could hear our mom's mom, Mamaw Grove, talking on the phone. "So is everybody okay? A girl? Do what? You are kidding?"

By the time Mamaw made it to question number three, Gil, Hallie, Orin, and me were standing around her wondering what she was doing at our house at four in the morning. And besides that, why was she on the phone, and who was she talking about? It all became clear when she said, "You mean there's *two* of them—two little girls?" From that moment forward, life took a drastic turn.

It was hard to believe that it had been three short years since they were born. I guess I stayed so busy that time just hurried away.

On this particular birthday morning, I got up right after Dad had left for work. He had been working on a barn that was about an hour from the house, so he didn't have to leave all that early. I wanted to get up so I could watch the morning farming report. I don't know why, but watching a couple of dry-talkin' farmers sitting behind a makeshift desk, talking and answering phone calls from desperate farmers was always entertaining to me. It was then that I learned all of the big words that farmers used and it helped me follow along in conversations that Dad might get into with some other farmer. One time we were down at Gracie Brothers getting a filter for Ole Red when Dad and some other locals started talking about blue mold.

"You been noticin' any blue mold in yer fields, Arden?" one old fella asked my dad.

"No, we've been fortunate so far," Dad replied.

"Well, down the road, Jay Gladden has the worst case I've ever seen!" the old guy shouted.

The conversation continued on, and I stood recalling all that I had learned about blue mold on a special edition farm report they had one year. The blue mold was a disease that caused the tobacco leaves to get all spotty and brittle. It made the leaves really light, and since tobacco was sold by weight, it could be a real problem.

I couldn't help putting in my two-cents' worth. "They say that the little mold spores can travel in the air and on farm equipment. They also said you should be careful taking equipment from an infected field to another field because you can spread the mold."

Both Dad and his toothless friend smiled. Dad rubbed my head so I knew I had said something good. Well, back to the birthday.

That morning the farm report was focusing on ways to control weeds in the tobacco. I listened closely because I knew that even when the tobacco didn't seem to be growing, the weeds never stopped. I was only about halfway through the show when Starr came walking down the hall. Her hair stood up as if she'd been electrocuted. Her eyes were half closed as she plopped down in the chair opposite of me.

"Happy birthday, Starr," I whispered.

"Happy birthday? Oh yeah! Happy birthday!" she squealed.

At that, she sprang into action and ran down the hall. She reminded me of Paul Revere and how he rode through the little towns in Massachusetts shouting, "The British are coming! The British are coming!" Starr wasn't calling out the militia, but she sure did get the rest of the family up.

"Happy Birthday!! Happy Birthday!!" she shouted as she ran.

Tempest was the first to join in the celebration. They ran throughout the house celebrating. The day was only a few minutes old, and already it was great.

Mom made us all special pancakes that morning. There wasn't a moment all day that we weren't reminded it was Starr and Tempest's birthday. Mom had made them each a shirt that said *Birthday Girl*, and they sported around the house in them all day. When Dad got home, we would have a party. Gil and Hallie helped Mom prepare. They hung up a few balloons and streamers. This only added to the excitement.

Orin and I had to mow the grass that day. I did not like mowing grass. It seemed like a waste of time and good cow food. I never understood why the grass in our yard seemed to grow even during the worst of droughts, but our pasture and hay ground grew oh so slow. We took turns mowing the yard with a push mower. We also took turns using the weedeater. We'd trim around the trees and flowers. Orin would always whack down Mom's flowers: "But they looked like weeds!" he'd say.

Dad came home early that day. It was only three thirty when he pulled up. He messed around with something in the back of his truck before he came to the door. "Where are the birthday girls?" he yelled.

Starr and Tempest ran to the door and collided with Dad. Dad bent over and hugged their little heads. "Are we going to have a party or what?" Dad asked.

We all got excited. Dad always knew what to say to get us excited. Mom and the girls had fixed a fine meal and the girls even baked a cake for the twins. Dad's parents, Mamaw and Papaw Merry, came to the party and so did our mom's parents, Mamaw and Papaw Grove. Even Mr. Malone came. We had dinner together, but Starr and Tempest rushed us because they wanted to eat cake and open presents.

The cake that Gil and Hallie baked had two little happy faces made with icing on it. They didn't do half bad. There were three candles on each end of the cake. Three for Starr, and three for Tempest. When the candles were lit, we all sang Happy Birthday to the twins. As soon as the last "You" of the song was belted out, Starr and Tempest let out hurricane force winds and extinguished the flames. Small streams of smoke were still rising off the candles, and Orin and I were licking the icing off from them. We each had some cake and ice cream.

Then came time to open presents. Even I was excited, and it wasn't my birthday. Each time the girls opened a present they squealed and hugged each other.

"Look!" one would say.

"Look!" the other would echo.

Needless to say, both gifts were alike. Everybody made sure that everything they got was the same.

They received a total of 10 dollars each from our Papaws and Mamaws. Gil and Hallie had made them a pillow. Orin and I gave them a couple of field mice we'd caught at the barn and placed in a coffee can. Tempest was so excited I thought she was going to squeeze their little eyes out. Mom and Dad always saved their gift for last.

"Well, girls, go open your last gift," Mom said as she pointed to something covered with a bed sheet.

Wasting no time, they ran over to the concealed gift and yanked the sheet off.

"A baby table and chairs!!" Tempest screamed.

Dad had asked Mr. Malone to make the twins their own personal table and chairs. They were always playing with dolls and now they could have tea parties like all little girls do.

We were all lost in the moment.

"Well, I didn't think it would be right for the twins to get all of the attention today," Dad said.

"What do you mean?" Hallie asked.

Dad replied with a smile, "I mean that I have a gift for each of you as well."

"You do?" we asked in unison.

"Yes I do. And they are in the back of my truck," he replied.

We all took off running for the truck.

"Be sure to get the one with your name on it," Dad yelled from behind us.

Only because he pushed us out of the way, Orin made it to the truck first. I was the last to arrive. As I drew near the back of the truck I couldn't help but notice that Gil, Hallie, and Orin were standing in manner that reminded me of when John outran Peter when they were running to Jesus' tomb. Just like John, they stood there, only looking.

Instead of running to the back of the truck, I stepped up on one of the rear tires and peered over the side. Lying in the back of Dad's truck were four new gooseneck hoes. There was a tag on the handle of each hoe that revealed the name of the new owner. I couldn't believe it, but then again I could. Dad was always good at getting us excited, as I stated earlier.

By now Mom, Dad and the rest of the party were standing on the porch. They were all laughing. I guess Dad had told them what he was going to do.

We each grabbed our gift and made our way to the porch.

"Mine doesn't fit my hand," I joked. "Can you take it back?"

The laughter continued.

What a moment: Mom, Dad, Mamaw and Papaw Merry, Mamaw and Papaw Grove, Starr and Tempest in their "Birthday Girl" shirts, and Mr. Malone all laughing on the porch above us.

Mr. Malone put his hand to his ear. "Do y'all hear what I hear?" We all stood attentive. "It sounds like little tobacco plants crying, 'Help Help! The weeds are getting us! You kids had better get to choppin'.'"

He was such a quiet man, but he sure knew how to make others make noise.

Despite the fact that the joke was on us, we each joined into the laughter.

They just don't make days like that anymore.

15

One Row at a Time

The heat of summer always seemed to creep up on us just about the same time the weeds started to grow in the tobacco. Dad wasn't joking when he bought us the new hoes. He meant for us to use them. We did have to wait a few days to break them in because we still had one acre of tobacco to set. We did it the day after the twins' birthday party. I never did look forward to choppin' out the weeds, but no matter how much I hated it, I knew I'd have to take part in the fun.

We usually chopped the tobacco out in the order that we planted the fields. Little weeds popped up out of nowhere in the fresh soil. You'd think you'd be able to see the seeds laying on the ground, but they always went undetected. We started in the field nearest the house, the one we'd pegged.

Gill, Hallie, and I made it to the field before Orin. He had gone frog giggin' the night before with some boys down the road, so he'd slept in. I wanted to get started as early as I could so I could beat the midday heat.

The hoe handle was about as tall as I was. I had to be extra careful when I chopped the weeds down. They seemed to grow as close to the tobacco plant as they possibly could. When they were growing extra close to the plant, it was best to bend over and pull the weed up by its roots. There were times when I tried to get by without bending over. I would oh-so-carefully place the hoe extra close to the stem. But there were also several occasions where I cut into the side of the tobacco stem. When I did this I'd bend over, pretending to pull weeds, only to prop up the injured plant with some loose dirt so it appeared that nothing had happened. It looked okay at the time, but it was only a temporary fix. As soon as the sun began to shine on the little plant, it started to wilt. After only a short time it was obvious I was guilty of several counts of plant slaughter.

When Dad returned home from work later in the evening, he would use Ole Red and a set of one-row cultivators to remove the weeds from the bulk. The bulk was the space between each of the rows. It was then that he'd notice how much damage we'd done. In the scheme of things, though, a few plants sacrificed for the good of all wasn't so bad.

Each of us chopped in a different row. There were twenty-four rows, and that meant each of us had to chop at least six rows. Sometimes, if I was lucky, Gil or Hallie would feel sorry for me because I was smaller and they would help me out. I always knew that there would be a day when I'd do the same for Starr and Tempest.

I had chopped one full row and was halfway through my second when Orin finally emerged from the house. The morning sun was at his back as he walked toward the field. The light shining through his red hair made it look like his head was on fire. I couldn't help but laugh.

No one really spoke as we chopped because we all chopped at different speeds, so there was really no one close enough to talk to. Just the sounds of creation and the scraping of my hoe cutting through the dark Kentucky soil could be heard. Just before I finished with my second row something shimmered as my hoe made contact with the soil. I quickly bent over to find a Liberty dime. I dropped my hoe and began to clean the dime on the tail of my shirt. I spit on the coin so the dirt would come off a little easier. After some scrubbing, I revealed the date. It was a 1944 Liberty dime and the oldest coin I'd found in the field.

"What are you doin' playin' in the dirt?" Orin sleepily shouted.

"I'm not playing. I just found an old Liberty dime," I replied.

Orin dropped his hoe and walked over to where I was. I handed him the dime, and he inspected my find. "Man, that old dime is in good shape. You lucky dog," he said as he hit me in the arm.

I took my dime back and put it deep in my pocket. Orin returned to his row watching his step just in case there may be a coin or something to pick up.

The morning passed swiftly. By noon we had chopped out the field. It was a good feeling to have the work finished, but my hands ached with blisters. Every summer I got blisters from chopping tobacco and other jobs we had to do. After you got the blisters once in the summer, they usually turned into calluses so you usually didn't get them again. Orin and I had both picked up a couple marbles, and Orin had even found an arrowhead. Other than a small chip in its side, it was perfect. We loved the treasures we'd found.

As soon as we ate a small lunch, the four of us, along with Mom and the twins, went to our farm pond to fish for a while. The pond wasn't a whopper, but it was the home of some whoppers. We turned over rocks and pieces of wood to find some red worms to use as bait. I never understood it, but you could always find them near dried-up cow piles as well. It always grossed the girls out when Orin and I turned over the cow piles to find worms.

We made our way to the pond and Orin was the first to get his line in the water. Hallie and I quickly followed. Gil helped Mom get a pole ready for Starr and Tempest. Soon we all had lines in the water. Little newts would come to the surface and bump our floaters. Hallie's floater began to jump up and down. Little by little, the tugs got stronger until the floater was pulled all the way under. Hallie did just what a good fisherwoman would. She waited until the floater was under and pulled to set the hook. By her expression and the effort she was putting out, I could tell her catch was a nice bass. We all watched as Hallie pulled in a bass about 12" long. It was beautiful—mostly green with white speckles. Starr and Tempest handed off their poles and came running.

"Oh, look at the big fish!!" Tempest yelled.

They were so cute when they were excited.

"Can I touch it?" Starr asked with big eyes.

"Sure you can," Hallie answered.

Both of the twins squealed as they poked the fish. They watched in wonder as Hallie put the bass back in the water. The fish sat stunned for just a moment, then darted off.

"Why you not keep it?" Tempest asked in broken three-year-old English.

"We only keep really big bass," she replied.

We actually had an unwritten rule that said you couldn't keep a bass out of the pond unless it swallowed the hook or was a whopper. A whopper, by Dad's definition, was a fish big enough to swallow your hand. Hallie's catch was nice but not a whopper so it had to go back in the water.

"Starr! Come and get your pole! You're getting a bite!" Mom shouted.

The girls rushed over and grabbed their poles. Tempest watched as Starr's floater disappeared. Mom helped Starr set the hook and Starr began reeling in the fish. At the same time, Tempest's floater, without warning, took a quick dive. Gil set the hook. For a short time, both Starr and Tempest were reeling in a fish at the same time. They were serious when they had a fish on the line, but when the fish got close enough to the bank for them to see, they really got excited. They each had caught a really fat hybrid bluegill. If you were just an onlooker, you would have thought we'd struck gold. Mom took the fish off the hooks and put them in a five-gallon bucket that we had brought along to put our keepers in. The fish splashed around in the bucket for a bit, then calmed down.

The twins didn't fish anymore but instead watched the fish in the bucket.

We stayed at the pond until we had caught twelve nice bluegill. Orin would fillet the fish, and Mom would cook them for supper. We'd barely made it back to the house when Dad pulled into the driveway.

"We're gonna have fish for supper tonight," I shouted to Dad.

He just smiled and came walking toward us. Starr and Tempest ran to him and wrapped their arms around his legs. They stood looking up at him, telling him about their catch. He bent down to listen. Orin wasted no time. He went inside to get his filleting knife so he could get started. Dad knew it would be a while before supper was ready, so he went to the barn and hooked up the cultivating plow.

He let me drive Ole Red from the barn to the field, but he did the plowing. When you plowed the tobacco for the first time each season, someone had to follow the plow in order to uncover any plants that might get covered. It only happened once in a while but every leaf on every plant was important. There was also the ever-present possibility that you might find some treasure as well. Following the plow wasn't a hard task. In fact, Starr and Tempest even helped. I would point at a plant that needed to be uncovered, and they would run to it and slowly unearth the leaves. I actually liked that concept, but it didn't last long. They got bored and ran off to do something else. Each summer I realized that my responsibilities continually took the place of more and more of my play time. I guess that's part of growing up.

It only took a short time for Dad to plow out the little plot. After he finished, he let me drive Ole Red back to the barn. That made me feel so big.

As we made our way to the house, we could smell the fish frying before we entered. Mom had fried the fish that we caught along with some frog legs that Orin had brought in the night before. She also fixed cornbread. Cornbread was an essential part of our diet and, according to Uncle Carve, it had been a staple of life for at least ten generations of Merrys.

Dad asked the blessing on the food, then we passed it around the table. Dad broke the silence, something he was good at. "Have I ever told you all how my dog Friday lost his eye?" he asked with a smile.

"No. You've only told us how he lost his leg," Orin said with a mouthful.

"Well, here goes," Dad said and began the story. "Friday's leg, or at least what was left of it had just healed up. He was learning to run pretty good, and then it happened. Jay Gladden had proposed to his girlfriend and they were going to get married. In those days when somebody announced they were going to get married, the whole community took it upon themselves to plan a reception or, as we called it, a "bellin'." A bellin' was a party unlike any other. People sang, danced, and anyone who had leftover 4th of July fireworks would let them off. There were even occasions where folks would shoot guns into the air. Anything to make noise. Well, Jay and his girlfriend had no more than said "I do" when the cow bells began to ring and gunshots were fired. I know it sounds crazy, but it was typical when I was a youngin'. Friday and all of the other dogs in the community loved bellin's because there was always some hog fat or other leftovers given to them. Friday had just begun chewing on a hunk of fat when none other than old man Tipton whipped out a rusty pistol and carelessly fired a series of shots into the air.

"BANG BANG BANG BANG BANG-PING!

"The first five shots were okay, but shot number six hit an unidentified object and began to ricochet off everything around. Everybody was yelling and falling to the ground and after at least a dozen glances, it happened. Friday let out a yelp reminiscent of the yelps he let out when he blew his leg off. He ran in circles. When I was finally able to catch him, I discovered that old man Tipton's sixth shot had put Friday's eye out. I felt bad for Friday, but I didn't want to spoil Jay's party so I quietly disappeared into the night, took Friday home, and bandaged up his eye. Everyone swore he'd die, but he not only survived, he attended bellin's for the next ten years of his life. So there you have it. That's how Friday lost his eye."

"What happened to his tail? He only had a nub, didn't he?" I asked.

"Oh, let's save that story for another time," he replied.

And that is just what we did.

16

A Midsummer's Day Dream

The fact the tobacco continued to grow despite the hot dry conditions was nothing short of a miracle. In fact, tobacco thrived during this type of weather. We had chopped the weeds from all of the fields twice by the end of June.

The second time we chopped and plowed the crop, we also dropped a small handful of ammonium nitrate next to each plant. We called this "side dressing the tobacco." Ammonium nitrate was a potent nitrogen fertilizer that really made the burley grow. It looked like little white BBs, and it burnt like fire when you got it in a cut. When we dropped it next to each plant we had to be careful not to get any on the tobacco plant because it would burn the plant and sometimes even kill it. There had been one good shower of rain since we finished side dressing the tobacco, and the plants were getting greener and stronger.

Throughout the month of July, the tobacco pretty much did its own thing. It just grew. This gave us time to tend to other things around the farm such as the garden, hay, and, of course, swimming. That is, if we got all of our work done.

Now you must understand that everything on the farm needed a little attention once in a while, even the cow pasture. There was one task that Dad made Orin and me take care of each July that I despised deeply. There seemed to be nothing good about it. The task was not only time consuming, painful, boring, and frustrating, but to top it off, it seemed that Dad would schedule this task for the hottest July day, a day so hot that the chickens laid fried eggs. The job I am speaking of is cutting thistles out of the pasture. A thistle is an evil plant that has sharp thorns all over it. During the midsummer months it had a fluffy purple flower that formed near its top.

Dad made the dreaded announcement the night before: “Boys, I need you to cut all of the thistles out of the pasture.”

I dreaded it as much as the first day of school.

Orin and I got up bright and early that morning, wielding our garden hoes, and trudged up the hill to conquer our prickly nemesis. The pasture seemed eternally big, and the thistles appeared to be everywhere. One swift slice to the roots of the small ones was sufficient but sometimes you had to just chop, chop, and chop the big ones. Back and forth and up and down we’d go.

After a couple hours or so we’d always get frustrated and weary. “Where do all these stupid things come from?” Orin yelled as he sunk his hoe into a big thistle.

“I don’t know, but what I’d like to know is why do we have to cut them down every year and why do they keep coming back?” I replied.

We both agreed that complaining wasn’t going to get the job finished, so we began to work extra hard to finish that ever-dreaded task.

After the last thistle had been cut, we agreed the pasture did look a lot better. By then the sun was directly overhead, and it was hot. What better thing to do at a time like this than go to the swimming hole?

Down the road just a bit was a swimming hole. Actually, it was the same place that we filled the tobacco setter with water earlier in the spring. The swimming hole was in a shady cove where the creek made a sharp turn into the hillside and another sharp turn away from it. The sharp turn made sort of a whirlpool effect as the water flowed into the area. When the spring floods came, the swimming hole looked like a giant sink swirling round and round. The water carved out a nice hole about 6-8 feet deep. Now that the spring floods were long gone, and the summer heat had set in, this made the swimming hole the most popular place in the holler.

We would always do whatever work needed to be done in the mornings, but when it got nice and hot we'd go cool off for an hour or so each day. Since we had already finished chopping down the thistles, we were safe to swim the day away.

Most of the time it was just Orin and I, but occasionally Gil and Hallie would come along. Once in a while Mom would bring the twins down to splash around in the shallow water. A couple of summers back, Orin and I had managed to get a large rope up and over the limb of an old maple tree to use as a swing. We tied some big knots in the rope and we also took a piece of a broken tobacco stick and tied it into the rope as well to use for a handle. To make the best of the swing, you had to pull it way back up onto the hillside, grab the tobacco stick handle, and jump. Once you got the hang of it you could quickly get your feet up onto one of the knots and enjoy the ride. The actual distance traveled on the rope was no more than 20 feet, but when you're a kid, the ride seems to go on forever. Once we were over the deepest part of the swimming hole, we would let go of the rope and fall into the water. Orin had a fierce cannonball. Near the end of summer, when the swimming hole would start getting low, Orin was banned from doing cannonballs because it stirred the water up too bad.

We stayed at the waterhole for a couple of hours. About the time we made it to the road, Dad came home from work. He stopped, and we jumped into the back of the truck to ride home. Orin and I could see that Dad slowed down as he drove past the pasture. He leaned over in the truck seat while he was driving and inspected the hill we had de-thistled. I guess we did a satisfactory job because he nodded and kept driving.

"Orin," I said with a serious tone, "Why don't you ask Dad why we have to cut those thistles each year?"

"No way! You ask," Orin challenged.

I took a deep breath and answered, "All right, I'll ask."

I don't know why we made such a big deal out of asking because Dad would and could answer anything we ever asked. And he never got angry when we asked.

When the truck came to a screeching halt in the driveway, I jumped out of the truck ahead of Orin.

"It looks like you boys did a fine job getting rid of those pesky thistles," Dad said as he slammed his truck door closed.

"Thanks, Dad," Orin said.

"Oh yeah, Dad, by the way, there's something Orin and I would like to know," I said nervously.

"Okay, what is it?" Dad asked.

"Where do all of those thistles come from?" I blurted out. Before Dad could begin his answer, I fired two more questions. "Why do we have to cut them down every year? Why do they keep coming back?"

Dad turned back to his truck and reached into the front seat. He grabbed a New Testament and sat down at the base of an apple tree in the yard and began to read from Matthew 13:24-30 and 13:36-43. It was about a man who sowed some seeds and when they came up he realized that someone had planted bad seeds on his ground in spite.

After he finished reading, he looked up at us. "Well, boys, you see that pasture is sort of like a man's life. In the spring time the farmer knows the pasture needs some new seeds to replenish the hillside. The farmer is careful to choose the best seed and scatters it oh so perfect. The ground gladly accepts the farmer's gifts and the seeds germinate into healthy plants that will carry out their one sole purpose, to feed the farmers other friends, the cows. You see, the cows and the pasture grass are both important to the farmer, but they just look different and have different jobs."

"But Dad," Orin butted in, "you still haven't answered our questions."

Dad smiled and continued on. "Now, although the pasture is doing what is right and trusting in the farmer for watch care, it's always being introduced to other creatures and things such as birds, deer, and squirrels. Once in a while these other animals bring seeds that look a lot like the ones the farmer had brought earlier and leave them behind. Before you know it, there's a thistle growing in the midst of the good grass. If you leave the thistle, it will grow and produce thousands of seeds. If the good farmer does not rid the pasture of the thistles before the seeds mature, then its seeds will fly across the pasture and the pasture will have a real problem. The thistles will smother out the good grass. Soon the pasture will lose its beauty and won't do its job of feeding the cows. In order to keep the thistles from taking over, the farmer must take care of the pasture and cut out the things that are harmful. Let me remind you that the good farmer never gets rid of his faithful pasture or lets it go forever. He simply cleans it up and helps it to do his work better."

"So you mean we are helping the pasture to help other things when we cut those old thistles?" I asked.

"Why yes, you are." Dad took a deep breath. "Boys, I want you to know that you are a lot like this pasture, because you too have a job to carry out for the God of this world. All of those seeds the farmer sowed were the good things in life, and when those things are used correctly they can help others through this life just as the grass helped the cows. Now about the thistles: those thistles are the things in life that should not be partaken of, like bad language, drinking, drugs, and bad friends. If those things are allowed to stand and spread their ugly seeds, then your life becomes like the pasture ridden with thistles, and smothered with ungodly things. Remember to always ask God to remove these thistles from your life so you can do His work and help others. Most of all, never forget to continually call upon God to rid you of these thistles year after year because those bad things in life will always be here to tempt you and try to take root and take over."

Eyes of understanding and wonderment gazed at Dad. That day we realized that keeping the thistles cut was more than just cutting down the real thing. Only Dad could take such a rotten task and reveal the hidden meaning.

17

Bloomin' Idiot

The month of July was a lot like the fireworks we watched on the Fourth of July—there for just a moment and then gone. We went down to Gracie Brothers to see fireworks each year. They had been putting on a little fireworks show since they opened. They didn't have any more than a dozen big fireworks but for a whole evening we did nothing but let off fire crackers and little bottle rockets that Dad had bought for us.

When it was nice and dark, Gracie Brothers would light up the night with their display. I can still see the sparkle of the fuses as they burned closer to the firework and then *BOOM*, the firework would explode into flight. There was a pause for a few seconds and then, miraculously, every color of the rainbow scattered across the sky. The night air would be filled with the "Oohs" and "Ahhs" of the spectators. Starr and Tempest would squeal and jump up and down each time a firework would explode.

Despite the fact the fireworks brought a lot of joy to the kids of the area, some people complained about the commotion. You could hear some of the townfolk saying things like, "It's no wonder their prices are so high. They have to charge an arm and a leg to pay for all of these fireworks." I always tried to ignore such talk because I loved the fireworks. The 4th was probably the most exciting event during the whole month of July.

Near the end of the month small flowers that we called "blooms" began to emerge in the tobacco field nearest the house. The growing season had been relatively dry, but as I said earlier, tobacco thrives in dry weather. The plants were well over my head, and the biggest leaves were longer than my arms.

"Won't be long till we'll be toppin' the tobacco," Dad said one Sunday morning after church.

You see, when the tobacco began to bloom, it was a sign that the growing season was nearing an end. Each one of the plants had a bud that turned into a flower, and every one of those buds had to be broken out of the plant. That is what we called "topping the tobacco." You did this so that all of the growth would go into the leaves instead of going in the bud. This helped the tip leaves get more nutrients and made them longer and wider. You wanted this to happen because the tip leaves were some of the most valuable. When they were fully cured or dried, they'd be dark red and heavy. The bloom was a big cluster of pink and white flowers. They were kinda pretty, but we didn't let them hang around long.

Each year we'd wait until about one-fourth of the field started showing blooms before we topped it. If you did it earlier, you'd forfeit some much needed growth. If you waited any longer, you'd have to fight the suckers that would begin growing in between each of the top leaves and the stalk. Those awful suckers would grow faster than a purebred calf and would give you all kinds of grief. The suckers were like a little plant that grew between each leaf and the stalk, robbing the rest of the plant of the nutrients and growth. We called them "suckers" because they sucked the nutrients away from the leaves. When there were several suckers on one plant, that plant suffered badly—and so did the person who had to pull all of the suckers out.

Early the next morning, Orin and I entered the field nearest the house to top the tobacco. There had been heavy dew, and it shimmered on the hillside where the calves were running and playing. Our spring calves were getting big and before we knew it, it'd be time to send them to market.

I began topping the first row I came to. The little buds popped out of the plant with a sound like a string bean snapping. Dad had taught us to break the bud out just above a leaf that was at least ten or so inches long. At first I had to really look hard to find the right place to break the bud out but after a few rows I could simply reach and snap the bud out. My hand just seemed to find the right place.

There were a few spots where the tobacco plants were so tall that I couldn't reach the bud. Then I had to bend the plant over carefully and pull the bud out. There were also some times when the bud had grown really tough and woody. When you came to a bud like that, you had to get out your pocket knife and cut it out. I carried a little lock-blade that I'd received for Christmas the year before. This was one of the only times of the year that my knife was actually sharp. It was usually dull from whittling sticks and cutting whatever I found to cut. I had asked Dad to sharpen it the night before so I could cut out the tough blooms. It worked like a charm. There were only a few instances where I needed to use my knife. The rest of the time I just snap, snap, snapped my way down the row.

Of course, Orin was much quicker than me because he was taller. He rarely ran into a situation where he had to bend the plant over to top it. We had topped about twelve of the twenty four rows when we met in the middle of the field. Orin was going one way in the row next to me and I was going the other. We stopped to talk.

"Have you seen all of the humming birds?" Orin asked while putting up his arm to keep a humming bird from hitting him.

"Yeah! They've all gone crazy. One almost put my eye out earlier," I began to tell him. "I just reached up to break out a bloom and as soon as that bloom snapped off, a little humming bird that was apparently going to get a drink from the bud I broke out came to a screeching halt right at the end of my nose! There I stood, staring that little beast in the eye!" I finished.

Orin just laughed. The little birds continued to zing back and forth across the field. They'd fly from one bud to the next in search of some sweet nectar. The closer you got to finishing the field, the more dangerous it became because the birds had fewer blooms to choose from. You almost needed safety goggles to top the last few rows in each field.

We finished the field nearest the house a little after noon. Neither of us lost an eye due to an out-of-control bird, either. The little birds had disappeared. We knew they had gone to someone else's field. As far as I was concerned, they could do whatever they wanted—as long as they stayed out of my eyes.

Orin and I went to the swimming hole for a while. We knew that when Dad got home, he'd spray the tobacco we had just topped and he'd need us to fill the barrel with water for him. After we topped each field of tobacco it was necessary to spray it with a sucker growth retardant spray. It kept the suckers from growing back in the tobacco for about twenty-one days. It also helped the tobacco turn a beautiful golden color in the field. When those tip leaves turned gold, it was time to harvest the tobacco.

Orin and I made the best of the afternoon splashing and swinging.

Before we started walking home, we stopped by Mr. Malone's to check on that field of tobacco. Mr. Malone was sitting on his porch so we went over to talk to him.

"Hello boys." He waved as we approached. We waved back.

Mr. Malone lived in a little house that he and his wife raised their family in. His wife had passed away when I was a baby so I don't remember her at all. The house was well kept because everyone in the community helped Mr. Malone whenever he needed it. We had a seat on the edge of the porch.

"How are you today, Mr. Malone?" Orin asked.

"I've seen better days, but they were about forty years ago," he said with a laugh.

"We got started topping the tobacco today. We topped the half acre up at the house," I went on to tell him.

"It's hard to believe it's already time for toppin'," he replied.

"Dad said we'd wait at least a week or so before we topped the tobacco in your field. He said he didn't want it all getting ripe at the same time," Orin remarked.

"Your dad is a smart man because a lot of people try to do all of the topping and sprayin' at one time and then they end up in a pickle when all of their burley gets ripe at once." Mr. Malone leaned back in his chair. "Did I ever tell you about the time a city slicker named Simon Shelton moved here and gave tobacco farming a whirl?"

We both said, "No" at the same time.

"Well, Simon came from somewhere down near Florida. He had made a fortune somehow and wanted to try his luck in tobacco farming. He bought a farm outside of town. You know the one just on the other side of Smothers' store?" We both nodded. "That farm had a tobacco base of over twenty thousand pounds. Everybody tried to teach him little things to help him along, but ole Simon insisted in his big city voice, 'I am an educated man. I can figure out how to do this stuff.'

"We were tired of hearing about how capable he was, so everybody let him be. When it came time to plant, Simon hired a couple farmers from out in the county to come and help him set the ten acres in one day. He got it all planted. The next time we saw him in town he made the remark, 'I told you all that I could do it.' He walked away smiling.

"His smile didn't last long. One thing that Simon failed to consider was that if you plant the tobacco at the same time, you are going to have to harvest it at about the same time as well. He also failed to remember that there were a couple of months until harvest and the weeds were already starting to grow like carpet in each row. Poor Simon chopped and chopped. He even put up signs that read, *Help Wanted.* But all of the farmers in the area were now busy taking care of their own crops and didn't have time to help Simon.

"By the time the tobacco did start blooming, Simon had lost over eighty pounds from working and worrying. He was a sight to see. His clothes barely stayed on him he was so skinny. In early August his ten acres of tobacco began to bloom. Within a few days the field was in full bloom. A week later, the field was still in full bloom. Simon had not cut out the first bud, so I went over to see what in tarnation he was doing. There was rumor that he may have worked his fool self to death. When I pulled up, Simon came walking toward me with a goofy grin on his face."

"'Have you ever seen a prettier crop of tobacco in your life, Mr. Malone?' he asked.

"'What do you mean pretty? That stuff is out of control. It needs to be topped!' I said as I jerked a bloom out of one of the plants.

"Simon grabbed my arm, looked at me half-crazed, and shouted, 'What are you doing? You are killing my tobacco!' At first I thought he was joking, but I could see sincerity in his eyes. So I sat down and explained to him the whole process of topping tobacco. Come to find out, he was planning on selling the pretty pink flowers to some big city florist back in Florida."

"Well, what happened to Simon?" I interrupted.

"Ole Simon Shelton did manage to salvage his crop and sell some burley, but the whole experience drove him back to Florida. I heard that he went back down to Florida and married that big city florist. He really was a bloomin' idiot," he finished with a laugh.

Orin and I burst into laughter as well. Just then we began to hear gravel popping under truck tires. Someone was coming up the road. It was Dad, so Orin and I said good-bye to Mr. Malone and ran out to the road to catch a ride. Dad stopped, and we jumped into the back.

That evening Orin and I filled the barrel for Dad as he sprayed the field nearest the house. This was a chore we'd repeat several times before each field was finished. Thankfully, Dad did space out the crops so that we too wouldn't look like bloomin' idiots.

18

Sengin' in the Holler

August was dwindling away. Since the waterhole became stagnant due to a lack of rain, we found other ways to occupy our time. We didn't have much time until the tobacco would be golden in the field and need to be harvested, but there was never a moment wasted on the Merry farm. One of my particular favorite ways to kill time was to go ginseng hunting. Although ginseng was its proper name, most people in the valley just called it *seng*. You might ask somebody where they were going and they may reply, "I'm goin' sengin'." The only folks who got lost in such a conversation were those from the city. To the rest of us, it was just common talk.

When you found a holler that had a good bit of ginseng in it, you kept it a secret. Sure, you are supposed to share, but seng is valuable. Dad always told us that the Chinese bought scuds of seng from Kentucky. He said they used it for medicine or something. Although I never did see a Chinese person at Smothers' store where we sold the seng, I took Dad at his word.

For the most part we would stay within a mile or so of the house when we went seng hunting, but when the price would go up for some strange Chinese reason, we'd go further.

On this particular day, Orin and I went just down the road to Mr. Malone's farm. He didn't care if we went diggin' seng on his farm, because he was too old to dig it himself and he knew that Dad had taught us to only dig seng after the berries turned a bright red and were ready to be planted. This helped to ensure seng in the holler for years to come.

Orin and I always took a lunch and a jar of water with us because a seng hunt could sometimes be an all-day ordeal. It was one of the few times when competition between us was friendly. We would walk until we found a dark holler, usually one filled with poplar trees, and our hunt would begin. We'd search the north side of each holler because that's the side of the holler that's the darkest, and seng loves the cool, dark side of the holler. It really was exciting to find a big, mature four-prong plant, but finding any at all was a thrill. The way you could tell if the seng was mature enough to be dug up was to see how many prongs or branches it had on its stem. There were one-prong plants. They were the youngest. There were two-prong plants. They were about 3-5 years old. Then there were the three-pronged plants, and last, the mature four-prong. Although both the three and four-prongs plants were mature enough to dig, the four-prong was the grandest find of all.

We had not been in the holler long when I spotted a few one and two-prong plants. To most people this wouldn't be much of a find but Dad had always told us, "Those one and two prongs have to have a Mom and a Dad plant somewhere." He also told us to always look uphill from the little plants because the seeds would most likely have rolled down the hill and sprouted below the parent plants. I looked up the hill just as Dad had taught us and, sure enough, there was a nice dark three-prong plant sporting a few red berries. I plucked off the berries and raked some leaves over them so they would sprout next spring and take the place of the plant that I was about to dig.

Before I would dig a plant I would always look at it carefully and admire just how perfectly it appeared to grow. Each one of the prongs had five leaves on it. There were three large leaves on the outside and two smaller leaves on the inside where the prong met the main stem. Sometimes the one and two-prong plants would only have three large leaves. Perhaps the neatest thing about the mature plant was the seed stem that protruded straight up between the prongs and displayed the beautiful red berries in nice neat rows. In late summer the seng plant would also develop a golden fringe around each leaf. This, just like with the tobacco, was a sign that it was time to harvest.

To dig the seng we'd use our pocketknife. You had to be really careful when you'd dig the seng because the roots were tender, and if you broke off a piece of the root it was like throwing money away. As I pulled away the dirt a wrinkly white root began to appear. Each root was different, which made digging it fun. After I had dug out the root, I picked up the top and held it like a bouquet because I always took them home. It was not uncommon to see a quart jar in our kitchen window filled with seng tops that Orin and I would bring home. We hated to leave the tops in the woods because they were so pretty and you couldn't do anything with them. Maybe the Chinese will find some important use for the tops one day.

Orin and I dug three and four-prongs all morning and then we decided to sit down and eat our meager lunches on an old oak log that lay on the ground decaying. As we began to chow down we were both awestruck by what stood before us. It was the biggest four-prong seng plant I had ever laid my eyes on. It was big enough to make Orin and I forget our hunger and fall on our knees next to the mammoth plant.

Four perfect prongs protruded from the stem and each leaf had a golden fringe. In the midst of all the leaves rose a stem covered with what seemed like a hundred bright red berries. They were all lined up neatly and glimmered in the sun. Neither of us really wanted to disturb this beauty, but we also knew that if we didn't dig it, someone else would.

"Have you ever seen anything like it?" I asked Orin, who was looking at the plant in amazement.

"Not in my lifetime but many times in my dreams," he answered with a laugh.

"We've gotta be extra careful with this root. No telling what it'll be worth," I said as I began to inch closer to the plant.

I began plucking the berries from the stem, while Orin raked back the leaves in a large area I commenced to plant all the seeds—one by one—and Orin covered them with a shallow layer of damp leaves. There were thirty-seven seeds on that one giant plant.

After we finished, we both clicked open our knives and began the excavation of the mammoth's root. As carefully as two archaeologists digging a fossil, we picked away the soil and watched as a giant root began to appear. The longer we dug, the more we were astonished. The root forked into two different directions. Orin went one direction and I went the other. It was no wonder the top was able to become so large and produce so many berries because the root was huge.

As the last bit of dirt was plucked away from the root, I picked up the stem that was still connected to the root and we both stood there in amazement. It looked more like a cluster of pawpaws than a seng root.

"Those Chinese won't know what to think of this monster, will they?" Orin said.

I was speechless. We began the long journey home with our dig that day. We both took turns carrying the big root—not because it was heavy, but because it was like a trophy for the Merry Brothers of Shady Meadows.

When we got home we emptied all of our seng roots into a coffee can. We had dug enough to fill one and part of another, and that was not counting the giant root. We carefully scrubbed each root with water and a toothbrush. The Chinese wanted their seng to be clean. We scrubbed roots for an hour.

Then came the time to clean the whopper.

"I wonder what this thing will be worth?" I asked Orin.

"I don't know, but I'll bet it'll be a fortune," he replied with a smile.

When we were finished, the roots were a beautiful display of tangled white on bath towels. We spread the roots out on the towels in the laundry room to dry. The sun shining through the window would cure the roots so that they could be sold. In order to sell seng roots, they had to be dried. It would be weeks before the seng was ready to sell, but it would be worth the wait.

That evening when Dad got home he assured us that the mammoth ginseng root was the biggest he had ever seen and it was possibly the biggest root to ever be dug in Kentucky. Only time would tell.

19

A "Sticky" Situation

As the end of summer break crept closer and closer, so did harvest time. Every farmer in the area had harvest on their minds. There were fewer patrons at both the Gracie Brothers and Smothers' grocery. Families were busy preparing for the hardest time of the tobacco-growing season.

Up until this point in the tobacco growing, the labor had been intense but nothing compared to what lay ahead. And since every farmer in the area would be busy with the harvest, there was rarely a spare hand in the valley. In fact, people came from all around looking for somebody to hire them. You'd see people you hadn't seen since last harvest time walking or driving from farm to farm looking for work. Most of the big farmers got the help. People like us just depended on the entire family for the workforce.

Before it was time to cut the tobacco, we had to be sure we had enough tobacco sticks to put the mature stalks onto. We had taken on Mr. Malone's base, so Dad knew we'd need at least 3,200 more tobacco sticks than last year. A farmer usually counted on the person that they leased from to already have a good cache of sticks provided. That was not the case for Mr. Malone.

Dad, Orin and I went down to Mr. Malone's to see how many sticks he had available. Dad couldn't believe what we found. The men Mr. Malone had hired to strip his tobacco the year before hadn't picked up any of the sticks after they took the tobacco off them. The sticks were strewn everywhere. Worst of all, a majority of the sticks had been tossed into the upper shed of the barn that was also used as a winter shelter for Mr. Malone's cows. The cows, not knowing any better, had trampled the tobacco sticks into tobacco stubs.

"What a shame," Dad said under his breath. "A man just can't get good help anymore."

We gathered up the sticks that were usable and found that only about 800 were still good.

"Dad, if we know we're gonna need more sticks, then where are we gonna get them?" Orin asked.

"I know Gracie Brothers sold out last week, but they only had those fancy sawed sticks. I like those rived sticks that Billy Whittle makes better," Dad replied.

Billy Whittle. What a name. Billy Whittle was an old bachelor who lived in the next holler over. He literally carved out a living from the trees on his farm. He was known the whole area over as the wood carvingest man alive. Speaking of carve, Uncle Carve told us that Billy was working on a porch swing one time and while he was etching some intricate design in the back, he cut himself wide open. Uncle Carve said that it was an awful cut, but Billy Whittle didn't even get excited. He picked up a handful of sawdust and held it to the cut. Uncle Carve said the blood soaked into the sawdust, turning it a dark red color. Billy just kept reapplying the sawdust to the wound and after a while, the cut stopped bleeding. Billy finished the swing as if nothing had happened. Uncle Carve swore from that day forward that Billy Whittle had sawdust in his veins, and that was why he loved working with wood so much.

That same afternoon, Dad, Orin, and me went around to Billy Whittle's place. You could tell Billy's place from anybody's because there was sawdust and wood chips and wood carvings everywhere. When we pulled up to the Billy's house there was a big bear that Billy had carved from the stump of an oak tree that used to stand near the drive. As we were stepping out of the truck we were greeted by his dog, "Old Hickory." Kind of a fitting name, don't you think? I patted Hickory on the head.

We heard pounding coming from the barn, so we headed that way.

As we approached the barn, Billy came into view. He was hammering a riving fro through a piece of red oak. A riving fro was a tool that resembled a hatchet, and it was used to split apart the large pieces of wood into slender tobacco sticks.

"Hey, Billy," Dad shouted.

Billy turned and greeted us. "Arden Merry, how are ya doin'?" he said with a smile.

"I'm doing great. I'm just out lookin' for something for my boys to do, and I'm gonna run short on sticks," Dad said as he shook Billy's sawdust-covered hand.

"Well, you came to the right place if you like good old-fashioned rived sticks. They'll put yer boys in a sticky situation all right," Billy replied while pointing to a mountain of seasoned rived sticks.

There must have been a hundred thousand sticks all stacked up in the lower shed of that barn.

"You better believe I want those rived sticks 'cause that burley doesn't hang onto those sawed sticks as well," Dad answered.

"Yeah, they're a little rough on the hands for the first couple of years, but they'll outlast any sawed stick you can find," Billy went on to say.

A lesson that all kids who grew up in a tobacco growin' family was that the rived sticks were splinter traps and that was why the tobacco clung to rived sticks better than sawed sticks.

"How many do ya need? Twenty or thirty thousand?" Billy asked jokingly.

"No, just about 2,500 for now," Dad replied.

I hoped I'd never see the day that we'd need twenty or thirty thousand sticks for anything.

Dad and Billy struck a deal and Billy let Dad have the sticks for fifteen cents apiece. I knelt down and figured out the price in the dirt.

2,500
x .15
$375.00

Three-hundred, seventy-five dollars' worth of splinters. Dad wrote Billy a check and then backed the truck up to the barn so we could load the sticks. Billy already had the sticks bundled in fifties, so it made counting a little easier. I struggled to get a bundle to the truck. Orin, Dad, or Billy would take my bundle and toss it onto the truck. As I tugged my first bundle toward the truck, I got a nice seasoned oak splinter between by thumb and my pointer finger. After I handed my bundle over, I put my hand to my mouth and pulled the splinter out. It hurt just as bad coming out as when it went in. I just kept wiping the blood onto my jeans. I'd have to get tougher because there was going to be a lot of stick handling in the next few weeks.

We finished loading the sticks, said our good-byes to Billy Whittle, and started home.

"Why did you buy 2,500 when we only needed 2,400 sticks?" I asked Dad.

"I figured I'd better buy an extra hundred while Billy had plenty," Dad replied.

"You mean you think he'll sell all of those sticks he had piled up?" Orin asked in surprise.

"In about a week or two every farmer in the area will be visiting Billy Whittle to buy tobacco sticks to replace all of their broken or missing sticks," Dad said with a nod.

We pulled up to Mr. Malone's barn and unloaded the sticks into the entry of the barn.

"There's no need to put the sticks in this field until we finish the field up at the house," Dad remarked.

Orin and I knew that meant we were going to put sticks in the field by the house that afternoon. Year after year Dad got us started putting the sticks in the tobacco, then left us to finish the job. Dad backed the truck up to the barn and we loaded what Dad thought would be plenty of sticks for the half-acre nearest the house. We had set that field first so it was the first to mature. The tip leaves were turning a bright golden color that resembled the leaves on a maple tree in the fall. That golden color, just like the golden color on the ginseng plant, meant that it was time to harvest.

After loading the truck, Dad drove it to the lower end of the field, and we began putting the sticks in the field. The tobacco would be put onto the sticks in just a few days and we'd take the sticks of tobacco to our barn to dry. We only had to put sticks in every other row, and since there were only twenty-four rows that meant there would be twelve stick rows in the field. The tobacco was nice and even, and the leaves were thicker than paper.

"This stuff ought to weigh good. These cool nights we've been having have made the leaves thick," Dad remarked as he examined a plant. "We'd better just put five plants on each stick."

In order to make sure you put only five plants on a stick, you had to put a stick between every second and then every third plant. So you had to count 2, 3, 2, 3, and so on. It could get a little confusing, but once you got the hang of it, it wasn't so bad.

As usual, Dad got us started, then went off to do other tasks that needed tending. Orin and I were left to put the sticks in the field, but I was not complaining because the hardest work was yet to come. And the fact that school was going to be starting after Labor Day was enough to make me sort of enjoy the work we were doing. I tried not to think about school.

Thankfully, the sticks Orin and I were putting in the tobacco were old and the splinters were worn away. Well, of course not all of the splinters were gone, but there were fewer when compared to the ones we'd be putting in Mr. Malone's field. If I was not mistaken, these were some sticks that Billy Whittle had sold Dad back when Dad took up tobacco farming. Billy sure knew his sticks.

We finished the field just before dark. The whippoorwills were singing away, their voices echoing off from the hillsides. They were always my favorite nighttime sound.

As Orin and I walked up the road toward the house he looked at me and said, "There has to be an easier way to do all of this stuff."

By "stuff" I knew that he meant sticking and cutting tobacco. The wheels in his mind had begun to turn, and I knew that when they began to spin, some ingenious idea was about to spring forward. I would just have to wait and see what he would think up.

When we got closer to the barn, the whippoorwills were drowned out by the rasp of a file sharpening something. Orin and I both knew that sound anywhere. Dad was sharpening the tobacco knives and spears. Dad always liked to be ready. I noticed that Dad only had out two knives and two spears. I remembered that Dad had told us earlier in the year that he was going to rely more heavily on Orin and me.

Orin and I both knew why there were only two knives and spears sharpened. One was for me and the other was for Orin.

"There's gotta be an easier way," Orin said as we watched Dad. "There's gotta be an easier way."

20

Technology

If there ever was a family that was not "high tech," it was ours. It seemed that everything we owned was old-fashioned and that was the way we liked it. But Orin and I did like the thoughts of more high-tech farm equipment and anything else high-tech that would make work easier.

Once we took an old bicycle and hooked it up to the hand crank corn sheller and, let me tell you, we could shell enough corn in fifteen minutes to do us a week. We just decided one day that there had to be an easier way to make that old hand crank sheller turn. At that moment our spark of ingenuity was so bright that it could have set off a powder keg. We just took the handle off the sheller, screwed a bicycle cog on it and then all we had to do was get on and pedal. One of us would pedal and the other would drop ears of corn into the sheller. Of course I was the one who always got stuck with dropping the corn in.

Orin would get on the bike and pedal like he was in some sort of race. I was extra careful when I was dropping the corn in the sheller because I could only imagine what it would do to a feller if he was to get caught in it. Ear after ear, the corn was shelled in record time.

There was also the time that we dug a diversion ditch that led from the creek and through the chicken lot in order to eliminate the need to water the chickens daily. "It's sheer genius, Sean. Just think. The water will just run in and the chickens can drink all they like. No more watering the chickens," Orin said with confidence. As always, I took him at his word. In fact his idea did work great until...

We had a pop-up thunderstorm. Not just any thunderstorm, but a real gully washer. Or, as Uncle Carve would call it, it was a real "Stump Jumper."

The rain was coming down in buckets, and our small stream running through the chicken pen had turned into a raging sea. Chickens were swimming, which is something chickens don't do well, and there was pandemonium in the henhouse. Luckily there was enough room on the roost for most of the chickens to survive. Yes, I said most. We stood and watched in horror as some of Mom's Dominicker's washed down the creek. Sometimes technology comes with a great price.

On this particular morning we were faced with a much tougher job than shelling corn. The burley had ripened in the field nearest the house, the same field that we put the sticks in the day before and it had to be cut.

Now came the hard part. We had to cut the tobacco all by ourselves because Dad was helping Mr. Malone get some logs off from the hill. Dad never missed an opportunity to test out Ole Red, and Billy Whittle had told Dad the day before that he needed some nice straight red oaks to rive more tobacco sticks. Mr. Malone told Dad to get all the trees he needed to earn back what he had spent on the tobacco sticks.

I could tell as we walked out the door that Orin had been contemplating some newfangled idea. Maybe it would be sheer genius or maybe a total disaster. Only time would tell. He finally broke the morning silence as we were walking to the barn to get our tobacco knives and spears.

"You know, I've been thinkin'. There has to be an easier way to cut the tobacco," he stated.

"Yeah, I know. I asked Dad if we could cut the tobacco with the mowing machine and then go back and spear it later. He just laughed at me," I replied.

"A machine! That is exactly what we need!" Orin shouted.

I could tell the wheels were really turning now.

"Okay, let's see. What kinds of machines and tools do we have that could cut the tobacco?" Orin asked.

We went into the tool room and went through all of the possible mechanical devices that may meet our needs.

“A hacksaw and handsaw are out of the question. They are too old-fashioned,” Orin quickly stated as he saw me grabbing a handsaw from the wall.

“What about the chainsaw?” I asked as I held up Dad’s Woodsman’s Special.

“No. You’d still have to bend over and besides, it is too heavy,” he said.

Just then it seemed a ray of the heavenly sunlight that we sang so much about at church was shining down on the weedeater. We both looked at it, and then we looked at each other and smiled.

“That’s it! It will be perfect! No bending over, and if we put the brush blade on it it’ll zip right through those old stalks!” Orin seemed to say in one breath.

I took the weedeater off the wall and we put the brush blade on it. Of course we made sure the blade was good and sharp because those tobacco stalks were tough. I used one of Dad’s files on it until the edges were as shiny as the bottom of Smif’s food dish after he cleaned up the breakfast scraps. Orin filled the tank with the oil-fuel mixture and off we went to the field. It seemed sort of ironic that we were going to the field to “field test” our latest innovation. We must have looked silly walking down the road to the field. Orin had the weedeater, and I was carrying a tobacco spear. As we walked, I could just imagine how awesome it was going to be. We were going to clearcut that field like a patch of thistles.

As we approached the end of the field, I have to admit, I had the butterflies. We were on the edge of a technological breakthrough. How could it be that no one had ever thought of this before?

“Let’s see how it goes,” Orin said with a twinkle in his eyes. Of course, he was going to be the one to just hold the weedeater and I was going to be the one to spear the tobacco onto the stick. Orin primed the little two-cycle engine and with a few cranks the brush blade began to spin like a top.

We walked up to the first plant in the row and Orin sank the blade into the plant. The stalk was no match for blade. It cut as clean as a whistle. I just picked the plant up, speared it, and *voila!* Just like that, we were underway. The weedeater made sort of a ringing sound as it cut through the stalks, and as I speared the tobacco it made a whoosh sound.

PING-WHOOSH-PING-WHOOSH-PING-WHOOSH...

Just like a nifty little machine we worked our way down the row. I guess Orin wasn't satisfied with the speed at which we were progressing, so he started speeding up. I could hardly get the stalk speared, and there was another falling. Then it happened.

Orin made a swipe at what he thought was a stalk holding up a tobacco plant but instead hit one of the stalks that I was walking around on.

"You hit my leg!!!!" I screamed in sheer panic. I reached down to grab my ankle. I just knew he had cut my leg clean off just above the ankle.

Orin shut off the weedeater and knelt down next to me. I could tell he was worried. "Are you okay?" he asked, wide-eyed.

"I think so. But I don't know how bad it is," I replied.

I was afraid to take my hand away from my ankle so I slowly untied my boot with my other hand. Orin pulled my boot off. It was obvious by the gash in the side of the boot that I had done a good job sharpening the brush blade. I winced with pain because the blade had tobacco juice on it and that stuff burned when it got in a cut. I looked at Orin and then slowly pulled my hand away from my ankle. Instead of a gaping, gushing wound, we found that the blade had only broken the skin. I never felt so relieved in all my life. Although he never said so, I know Orin was relieved too. Can you imagine what it would have been like for him to explain to Mom and Dad how he cut my leg off?

"I didn't know that technology had to be so painful," I said with a half grin. Orin just laughed.

We both looked back down the row that we were cutting and realized that this particular technological advancement had some safety issues that needed to be worked out before it was ready for the market. I didn't feel like we had totally failed because, after all, Miss Bass had told us that the Wright Brothers were not successful on their first try. I got up and hobbled to the house where I cleaned my cut. I don't know what hurt the worst: the cut, or the realization that Orin and I still had a field of tobacco to cut.

The rest of that day we cut tobacco. I know Orin was thinking the same thing I was that whole time. *Gosh, I know there has to be an easier way to do this. But how?*

No doubt, just like Wilbur and Orville, we would not give up. There would be a next time, and maybe just maybe, technology would prevail.

21

The Sunday of all Sundays

Two days of old-fashioned stickin' and cutting tobacco followed the day that would become known as the "Great Technological Flop." Of course Mom and Dad got wind of what had happened. They were both a little concerned that I might need a tetanus shot or something. But when they both saw my wound, scrape, whatever you want to call it, they broke out into laughter.

Orin didn't get into trouble because I was as guilty as he was. I was just the one who had to bear the scar...literally.

As I had stated earlier, school was going to reopen the day after Labor Day. Dad knew he was going to lose his workforce, so he always made Labor Day a day to remember. We would cut tobacco several days in advance to Labor Day, as long as the weather was permitting. That way the tobacco would be wilted and ready to house. When I say "house," I mean to be hung in the barn in order to cure or dry.

Of the three and one half acres that we had raised, we had been able to cut two and one half acres and get the sticks in the other acre. We had been busy little children and we had the splinters to prove it. Those sticks we had bought from Billy Whittle must have been extra splintery because it seemed I picked a thousand splinters out of my hands.

We had worked right up until dark on the Saturday before Labor Day getting things ready for the housing party. Before turning in for the night we pulled the two flatbed wagons out of the shed and left them next to the half acre nearest the house. Since we had cut this field first, we'd house it first as well. Dad just left Ole Red hooked to one of the wagons and left him out to sleep under the stars. Only Sunday stood between us and the work.

The next morning Mom awoke us with the sweet aroma of her pancakes. She never took any special orders that morning. She just made them all in the shape of tobacco leaves and coins. It was Mom's way of getting us pepped up for the big day.

After breakfast, Orin and I got dressed and walked to church. We walked past the fields of cut tobacco that we hoped to empty the next day. At one point in the road, you could see a large portion of Shady Meadows. As far as you could see there were fields of tobacco that were cut or ready to be cut.

As we approached the church building, there stood Brother Force. When he reached to shake my hand, he noticed the many splinter marks and cuts. "Billy Whittle ought to be ashamed of himself for selling such splintery sticks."

I nodded in agreement. Orin followed me in.

As we eased our way toward the front I noticed a head that seemed so familiar, but one I had never seen in church before. I pondered who it could be and then they turned around just far enough for me to make out who it was. I couldn't believe it. It was Miss Bass, and she was sitting next to none other than Billy Whittle. By now Orin had made the same discovery and was elbowing me in the ribs.

"Do you see what I'm seein'?" he asked while still staring at the couple.

Just then Mom, Dad, and the rest of the Merry clan came sliding in. Brother Leroy and Sister Paulie manned their stations and Brother Leroy belted out, "Let's turn to number 25, 'We'll Work 'til Jesus Comes.'" Sister Paulie commenced to playin', and the church commenced to singin'.

There was some irony in that song that day. Many of the people sitting in the congregation would be doing the same thing that the Merry family intended to do the next day. We'd all be workin' 'til Jesus comes all right. About noon tomorrow we'd all be wishing that Jesus would part those Eastern skies and take us to a place where they didn't grow burley.

Then the music stopped, and Brother Leroy said, "Let's sing number 215, 'When the Mists Have Rolled Away.'"

The irony would not stop. I was amazed at Brother Leroy's premonition of the day to come. But nothing amazed me more than what Brother Force said as he entered the pulpit that day.

"Friends, today is a great day. In fact, today is a special day. We have all come out to serve the Lord and, unbeknownst to most of you, you are also gonna witness a marriage ceremony."

My jaw nearly hit the hardwood. I felt like the walls of Jericho when all those people shouted and blew on the rams' horns. I nearly fell over. Everyone now knew why Miss Bass and Billy Whittle were sitting on the front pew. Nobody ever sat on the front pew. We all knew something was going to happen, but nobody suspected a wedding.

Brother Force stepped out from behind the pulpit and motioned for Billy and Miss Bass to come forward. Miss Bass nearly ran to the front. She was sporting a ring that would weigh down a good pickup truck. Billy must have sold a lot sticks to pay for that thing. Billy slowly stood up and walked toward Brother Force. I could have swore that there was a trail of sawdust following him all of the way to the front. They both stood there and took the vows of holy matrimony. Then Billy Whittle kissed Miss Bass, or should I say, Mrs. Whittle, in front of the whole congregation. It was the first time I had ever seen her smile. Maybe old Billy had whittled her some feelings. I hope he whittled her a sense of humor while he was at it.

Mrs. Whittle. Now that would take a little getting used to. *Just wait 'til everybody at school hears about this.*

After the ceremony, Brother Force preached a short message on nothing other than, "The Fall of the Walls of Jericho."

I was really distracted then. All that I could think about was poor old Billy and the peace that he once knew.

After the last "Amen" was said, we all went out the front doors to shout our congratulations to the Whittles. All of the way home Orin and me walked and talked about the service.

"Can you believe it, Sean?" Orin asked with big eyes.

"No. I'm still in shock about the whole thing."

"Can you imagine what kind of paddle Billy will cut out for Mrs. Whittle to use on you all this year?" Orin said.

"I hadn't thought of that! Man, I'll bet he'll make one that'll leave splinters like his tobacco sticks do," I said with a bit of fear.

The rest of the way home I pondered what the school year would hold for me and the other kids at school who had already gotten on the newly married Mrs. Whittle's bad side even before she became a Whittle. For a while I was able to forget about the hard day that lay ahead of us. Then the day just got weirder.

Orin and I had just started up the sidewalk when Billy and his bride pulled up. Mom and Dad had invited the newlyweds to dinner. How could I bear to eat with my old teacher?

By the time that Dad and Billy finished conversing over how good the tobacco growing season had been, Mom and the girls had already set the table. We made our way to the big table and Starr and Tempest sat at their little table. Dad asked the blessing on the food and we all dug in to a good home-cooked meal. Hardly anyone spoke for the first few minutes, then Billy chimed in.

"Arden, do you remember that old dog that you had when we were growin' up?" Billy asked with a mouthful.

"Friday," Dad answered.

"Yeah, old Friday," Billy said as gravy ran down his chin. I half expected him to reach in his pocket and pull out some sawdust to soak up the gravy but instead he acted like a civilized married man would and used his napkin to wipe his chin.

"Did you ever tell these youngins how your dog lost his tail?" Billy asked.

"I've never made it that far in the story," Dad answered. "Why don't you tell 'em, Billy?"

Billy began, "It was about this time of year, and everybody was itchin' to get their tobacco in. I'd been workin' like a mad man tryin' to fill all the orders I had for rived sticks. After I rived all the sticks I was gonna rive, I hired myself out to cut and house tobacco. Well, Mr. Malone hired me. That year had been a particularly bad year for copperheads and other snakes. A couple people had been bit just down the road. In fact, a big old copperhead is what put old man Tipton out of business. He was out stoking the fire on one of his stills and a copperhead latched right onto his hand. He grabbed the snake with his other hand. The snake let go of the first hand and bit the other. Tipton's hands swelled up like watermelons. After that his moonshine never was the same, and some big city moonshiner took all his business.

"Mr. Tipton wasn't the only person to get bit. Someone was bit the week before when they were housing tobacco. So when I went to work for Mr. Malone, I was on extra high alert for snakes. I was cutting my way down the first stick row when I bent over and came face to face with what appeared to be the fattest copperhead I'd ever seen. I stood up slowly and reared back my tobacco knife. I swung down at the serpent and, when I struck it, realized it was no snake at all. I had just cut Friday's tail clean off! He'd been out all night chasing rabbits and was resting in the shade of the burley. Let me tell you, that dog ran in circles for what seemed forever. When I caught him, I put a handful of sawdust on the end of his nub and after that he seemed okay."

"Is that really how Friday lost his tail?" I sincerely asked Dad.

"I am afraid so, son," Dad replied.

"Poor dog," Mrs. Whittle said.

"Poor indeed," Mom replied.

There were a few more harebrained stories that circulated around the table that day, but none topped the story of how Friday lost his tail.

Billy and Mrs. Whittle stayed at our house all day and even went to the Sunday evening service with us. That night after church, Orin and I talked before we went to sleep.

"If things get any more weird, I don't know what I am going to do," I said while leaning up on one elbow.

"You think things are bad for you. Can you imagine how poor old Friday must have felt?" Orin answered.

"Yeah I guess that you're right. But I still say this has been a Sunday of all Sundays," I commented just before I drifted off to sleep.

22

Just Hangin' Around

The moon must have moved extra fast across the sky that night. I awoke with the same thoughts I had fallen asleep with. I still didn't know who to feel the most sorry for—Dad's one-eyed, three-legged, bob-tailed dog, or Billy Whittle, who had just married my old teacher.

Anyway, everybody in our household was up before dawn. Dad believed in getting an early start and it was best to get as much of the tobacco out of the field before the sun was able to dry the dew off from the bottom leaves. Although the bottom leaves were classified as "trash," they were still quite valuable and worth saving. We ate as much as we could because only Dad knew when we'd break for lunch.

We each started the morning wearing long sleeves. The September nights were becoming cooler and cooler, but the days were still very hot. It wouldn't be long before we'd shed the long sleeves. As we walked down the field I could hear Smif running a cottontail in the holler below the house. That dog never stopped.

As with most of the chores on the Merry farm, Dad had formulated a job for every one of us. In this case I got off pretty lucky. I would spend a large portion of my morning driving Ole Red. When we were loading tobacco you had to keep Ole Red in first gear, low range, and no matter how much throttle you gave him, you could never go faster than one mile per hour. Since there was no real danger in me speeding down the field and out of control, Dad inducted me as the designated driver. My older siblings didn't like the fact that I had a fairly easy job but they also knew I would struggle carrying those big sticks of tobacco, so they didn't make much of a fuss. I never complained either because I knew that this would no doubt be my last year as the designated driver. It was no secret I was growing and growing fast.

Orin, Hallie, Gil, and Mom were the tobacco packers. They would carry each stick of tobacco to the wagon and hand it to Dad. Each stick had five stalks of tobacco on it. Dad was the all-time stacker. Nobody could get more tobacco on the wagon than Dad. He had built the wagons himself, so he knew what kind of loads he could put on them. You might be wondering about Starr and Tempest. Well, their job was to walk around the field and pick up any big leaves that may have been broken off the tobacco while it was being cut or packed to the wagon. Remember, every leaf is important to the tobacco farmer. I recall Hallie griping once about having to pick up the leaves.

"I don't understand why we have to pick up every stinkin' leaf that falls off," she griped.

"Those stinkin' leaves will be paying for your clothes and food for the next year," Dad replied in a tone that ended the argument.

When I fired up Ole Red, he let out a little more smoke than usual because of the coolness of the morning. But soon he was running like a scolded dog, or should I say a bob-tailed dog. I put the tractor in first gear, low range, and let the clutch out slowly. Just like a well-oiled machine, our family started down the field loading the wagon with burley.

One stick at a time, Dad stacked the tobacco in such a neat fashion. He had loaded so many sticks in his lifetime that he knew just how to place each stick so that it wouldn't fall off the wagon.

We crept down the outside rows of the half acre and when I reached the end of the field I turned Ole Red and the wagon around and we began going back the other direction. This time I went down the other side of the field.

Dad always tried to get at least 250 sticks on each wagon. We made a couple of rounds and then Dad gave me the signal to pull the wagon to the side and hook up the other wagon so we could fill it up as well. I did as Dad asked and soon we were back to loading burley. We made several passes around the field and soon the wagon was full. Now Dad took the wheel so he could pull the wagon into the barn. This was one of our favorite parts of the day because we got to ride on the back of the wagon. There was something special about riding on the back. Even Smif rode sometimes.

Dad took his time and made sure he had good clearance on each side of the wagon as he pulled the wagon through the barn. He stopped where he thought was best. Now came the hard part.

Our barn had been built in the 1930s and it was six tiers deep. The tiers were long poles that spanned the distance from one side of the barn to the other. They ran parallel to one another and the tobacco sticks filled with tobacco would be placed across them. The tobacco would be left hanging until it was completely dry. The top tier was at least thirty feet off the ground.

Hanging tobacco was not for those who were afraid of heights. It took four people up in the barn and two on the wagon. Dad stood on the bottom tier because he was the strongest and the person on the bottom had to handle every stick that was hung. Dad would pass the stick up to Orin, who stood on the second tier. From there he could hang tobacco on the second and third tier. Orin would also have to pass tobacco up to Hallie, who was standing on the third tier. She was responsible for hanging tobacco on the fourth and fifth tiers. Hallie would also pass sticks of tobacco up to Gil, who stood on the fifth tier. Gillian had a fairly easy job because she just had to hang tobacco on the sixth tier, but as I mentioned earlier she was nearly thirty feet off the ground. I stayed on the wagon to help Mom hand the tobacco up to Dad. Starr and Tempest had the job of stringing up the leaves that they had picked up onto wires. Although I was able to climb around on the tier poles—Lord knows I spent many hours playing on them and swinging from them—I still was not strong enough to hoist the tobacco into place. Once again, I did not complain because I knew that my day would come soon enough.

Mom and I started handing the tobacco up as soon as everyone was in place. The first stick went straight to the top. When you set the tobacco stick straddling from one tier pole to the next, you then had to spread each stalk apart so that each could get enough air to cure. If you didn't spread the tobacco apart the stems on the leaves would begin to rot. This was called "house burn," and it wasn't something you wanted because it could ruin the quality and weight of your leaves.

As we handed the tobacco up, dirt and grime fell into our eyes the whole time. I always tried to just raise the tobacco up without looking to see where Dad was. Most of the time I got it close enough to where he could grab the stick, but one time I hit his foot as I raised the stick and nearly knocked him out of the barn. I was a little more careful after that and would make a quick glance before I raised the stick.

Stick by stick the load was emptied. Soon it was time to bring in the second load. Then, the third, fourth, fifth, and then finally, we took a lunch break. It was not a long break, but it was still a break.

Mom fixed us her famous bologna sandwiches, and we dug in. Mom had made enough so we each could have two sandwiches. She always made sure we each had an oatmeal pie for dessert as well.

After only about a twenty-minute break, we went after another load. Dad had managed to get the half acre on three loads, and we had already gotten two loads from down at Mr. Malone's. By now my hands were sore from handling all those sticks. Everybody but Mom and Dad was showing some sign of fatigue. Despite our weariness, we still had miles to go. I think Dad could sense our need for rest so he drove extra slow back down to the field.

We pulled up to the field and began to load the wagon. We had just gone about halfway down one trip when Billy and his Mrs. pulled up. They both came walking up the field, hand in hand.

"What in the world are you newlyweds doing?" Dad asked.

"Blenda told me that she had never seen nor taken part in tobacco housin', so I told her I couldn't be married to no such woman. I figured instead of an annulment that I'd just put her to work instead," Billy answered with a grin.

Blenda. Her name is Blenda. Blenda Whittle. Now if that isn't a tough name to say five times.

"Well, you've come to the right place," Dad said as he pointed to all the sticks of tobacco waiting to be loaded.

Billy and Blenda just started helping the others hand the tobacco to Dad. I noticed that I was able to go a little faster since they started helping. We loaded two loads in record time. Now we were off to the barn. Dad wanted to put as much of Mr. Malone's crop in our barn along with the crop from home so that we wouldn't have to haul it to the house during stripping time. Dad said these would be the last two loads that we took up to the house and that the rest of the tobacco would have to be hung in Mr. Malone's barn.

I expected Billy and Blenda to go on back home, but instead they piled into Billy's pickup and followed us up the road. It looked kinda funny to see Blenda sitting in the middle of the bench seat. I thought that was something only teenagers did. I guess when you're in love you do crazy things.

Dad pulled the wagon into the barn, and Billy was the first to climb up into onto the tiers.

"Oh be careful," Blenda said with her hand over her mouth.

Billy saw this as a good time to show off, so he let go of one of the tier poles and dangled by the other. Blenda let out a scream and then must have realized that Billy was only foolin'.

Now that the Whittles were helping, that freed up two people. Gil and I gladly gave up our spots and began to string up the leaves that had fallen off the tobacco. There were several piles of leaves waiting to be strung up. We would wrap one end of a long piece of wire to a nail and then, just like stringing popcorn for the Christmas tree, we strung the leaves on the wire. Some of the stems were tough and pushing the wire through them was no easy task. Despite the challenge, it was better than the alternative. It seemed like no time had passed at all when Dad pulled the now empty wagon out and went to get the other that was parked at Mr. Malone's. Having two more grownups sure did help, even if one was inexperienced and the other was nothing more than a big kid.

Before darkness came over the valley that evening and just as the whippoorwills began to sing, we handed the last stick up to be hung.

"That's the last one," Blenda shouted.

One at a time, people started bailing out of the barn. By now, even Mom and Dad were showing signs of tiredness. Starr and Tempest had retired about an hour earlier. Gil took them to the house to get cleaned up for bed.

"Billy, I really appreciate you two coming over to help out," Dad said as he shook Billy's hand.

"I had to break her in right, Arden," Billy said with a laugh.

“It sure has been an experience, Mr. Merry,” Blenda said as she reached to shake Dad’s hand. “One I’ll not soon forget.”

“I’d say that every muscle in your body will remind you of what you did when you get up in the morning,” Dad joked.

Just then Blenda turned to me. “I guess I’ll be seeing you in the morning, Sean.”

I was speechless. Why did she have to remind me?

We eventually made our way to the house and, one by one, we showered and got our clothes ready for the first day of school. There were times when I had a strange flutter in my stomach the night before school that kept me from sleeping. Tonight I was sure that nothing, not even the thought of seeing Mrs. Blenda Whittle in the morning, would keep me from sleeping. Not after a family field day like the one we’d just had.

Nothing.

23

A Time to Rhyme

"Rise and shine, little boys." Mom's voice broke into my sleep like a bandit robbing me of precious rest. I was quick to rise because I didn't want to start off the new school year by testing Mom's waking ability. Orin was a little slower than me but faster than usual.

It really was hard to believe that summer break was over, and we were about to begin a new school year. This would be the first year that I would be the only Merry at Roy G. Biv Elementary. Orin was going to be a big freshman, Hallie would be in the eleventh grade, and Gillian was now a senior. Gil would have her hands full taking care of her studies and keeping her eye on Orin. I only imagined what kind of things he'd do at the high school.

Mom had already laid out my clothes. I had to get some new pants because I'd outgrown all of the pairs I wore in the sixth grade. I also had an arsenal of hand-me-downs from Orin. We were never too proud to wear what had already been worn. I slipped into my new clothes, brushed my teeth, and made my way into the living room. Mom was standing there with her camera in hand. She always took our pictures on the first day of school. We had to stand in the same spot each year. That way you could look at pictures from the past years and see how much you had grown. I never liked pictures and especially pictures at six in the morning. As soon as the flash stopped, we made our way to the bus stop.

Orin was the last to arrive. Boy, let me tell you, he had spent the entire morning making sure that he looked good for his high school debut. In the distance, we could hear Loretti going through the gears of bus number 41. She soon rounded the bend and came to a screeching halt. As always, we waited for the dust to pass before we crossed in front of the bus. I stepped onto the bus and, sitting in the driver's seat was not our "usual" Loretti but one who was refined. Her hair was a different color, and when she said, "Hello, Merry children," I noticed that she had more teeth than last year. She had been at church, but I guess I was so distracted by the big wedding that I didn't even notice. My, how things change over just one summer.

The bus rolled down through Shady Meadows passing field after field where tobacco once stood. I guess we weren't the only family in the field the day before. Several boys would probably miss school today, because they would have to stay home and help house tobacco, but Dad saw to it that we were in school. The rest of the crop could wait until the weekend.

It wasn't long before we arrived at Roy G. Biv. I was the only Merry to get up, which was kinda strange.

"You think you'll be okay without me here to watch over you?" Orin asked with a laugh.

"Oh, I think that I can handle my own," I replied.

I had barely stepped off the bus when Loretti sped away. I walked into the gym that was already buzzing with conversation. The first day of school was always interesting. So many kids had grown taller, and most had on something new and were sporting a nice summer tan. I sat down at a table where several of my classmates were.

"Guys, you're never going to believe what I witnessed just this past Sunday," I began the morning gossip.

"What'd you see?" the group asked in unison.

"You all remember Miss Bass?" I asked, knowing that they did. "Well, she married Billy Whittle!"

"She married the tobacco stick man?" my buddy Tal Smothers asked all big-eyed. Tal was the grandson of the Smothers that owned the store.

I just nodded my reply. Everyone was too shocked to speak.

"They tied the knot right in front of the whole congregation. It was a sight," I continued.

"Well, I guess that proves there really is someone for everybody," Tal joked.

"Speak of the..." I started as Mrs. Whittle came strolling in. There was actually a hint of a smile on her face and, not to mention, a shiny piece of seasoned hickory shaped like a paddle sticking out of her purse. I don't know what got the most attention—the hint of a smile or the paddle. I know my eyes were on the paddle.

"Well, who is our teacher gonna be this year, fellas?" Tal asked.

A small boy named Brooks gave us an answer that would come to haunt us for the next nine months.

"Miss Frances is the seventh-grade teacher this year," Brooks said without raising his head.

I couldn't speak but could only think about what I had been told about Miss Paris Frances. You can bet that her name was no coincidence. She always told how she was born unexpectedly while her parents were on vacation you know where. Yes, Paris, France. She was appropriately named for the occasion. Miss Frances was the most poetic person that one could ever meet. The year Orin had her as a teacher, nearly everything he said rhymed by the time he passed into the eighth grade. On a really good day she would not just rhyme but also sing. I could hardly wait to see what she might have us doing the first day. Orin had told me that if you wanted to get on her good side you had to do your best to rhyme and act all poetic. I didn't know how to act poetic, but I guessed I could give it a shot.

All of the teachers assembled in the gym at eight o'clock and called for their class. The kindergarten teacher called her class first. There were several little kids crying. I felt like joining them when Miss Frances called my name. After she called all of our names, we followed her to the last class in the hallway. She stopped at the door and motioned for us to enter.

The room was decorated with seemingly hundreds of European artifacts. Miss Frances made at least one annual trip to some part of Europe each year as a memento to her name and she would bring back souvenirs to decorate her room. There was a miniature Eiffel Tower on her desk, a model of the Globe Theater on a table, a matador's cape hanging on the wall, and countless other treasures.

There were little tags on each desk and you had to find the one with your name on it. Under your name was a small verse of poetry.

What was that all about? Everyone found their seats and Miss Frances made her grand entrance.

"Everyone up. It's time to *say* 'The Pledge of Allegiance' to start our *day*," she rhymed.

We stood and said the pledge.

"I am sure that you have noticed the verse on your name *card.* Read it and try to understand it. None of them are too *hard*," she rhymed again.

I silently read the verse that was on my card:

An unlearned mind is like a shallow stream;
A surface, a bottom and not much in between.

"Each of you is going to have to decipher what the verse means and when you stand to introduce yourself to the class, you are going to read and explain your verse." That time when she talked, she didn't rhyme.

I looked around and discovered that I wasn't the only student a bit worried. We had only been in class for five minutes, and we were already rhyming. I thought and thought about my verse, remembering the advice Orin had given me, and then it came to me. I jotted down what I thought the verse meant and readied myself to explain.

Miss Frances started in the first row and made her way up the second and back down the third row where I sat.

"Sean Merry, please *stand* and explain the verse that's in your *hand*," she rhymed.

I stood and cleared my throat. "My name is Sean Merry, and my verse reads:

An unlearned mind is like a shallow stream;
A surface, a bottom, and not much in between."

"That verse is one of my favorites, and 'tis so true. Now tell me, Sean, what does that verse mean to you?" she rhymed.

And so I plunged in to my rhyme:

"I read the verse, but at first, the answer did not appear.
The more I thought, the more I pondered, the answer became more clear.
Just like shallow water's no good for fishin', except for suckers and some carps,
An unlearned mind is not so deep when it comes to smarts."

I looked up, and there were tears welling up in Miss Frances' eyes. She broke out into jubilant applause. "That was wonderful, Sean! I think you may be a natural poet!" she shouted as she wiped her eyes. A teacher's pet had been born.

The rest of the day was a breeze. Miss Frances allowed me to pass out all of the papers and do all kinds of other chores around the room. It really was amazing how powerful poetry was in Miss Frances' class.

The day ended all too soon and before I knew it, it was time to pack up and go home. I had never had a first day go so swift or swell.

"Don't forget your homework! Be sure to take your *time!* And don't forget to list ten objects that with another *rhyme*," she rhymed one last time.

I stepped onto the bus, said hello to the new improved Loretti, and made my way to the back of the bus where Orin was sitting.

"Well, how'd your first day of high school go?" I asked Orin as I plopped down beside him.

"Good," he answered. "Who's your teacher this year?"

"Let's just say that it is rhyme time, and I am officially the teacher's pet," I replied with a smile.

"Let me guess. You swept Miss Frances off her feet with a rhyme right off the bat, didn't you?" he inquired.

"I did just what you said, and it worked like a charm," I replied.

Orin just smiled and looked out the bus window. I could tell he was sort of proud that he'd been right.

When Loretti turned up our holler, I was relieved to see that Dad and someone else had cut the last acre of tobacco at Mr. Malone's. All we had to do was wait until Saturday to house it. If I could survive the Labor Day blitz, I could survive one more acre of housing.

We rolled on until we reached home. I was the first one off the bus. I never wasted any time because I wanted to be home where I was free. We went into the kitchen where Mom had dinner ready. Both Starr and Tempest met us with a leg hug. They were so used to having us around during the summer that they actually missed us not being home.

After dinner, Orin and I went up to the pond to fish until dark. The water was cooling down, so the fish were beginning to bite again. We stayed until dark and made our way home.

Just before we turned out the lights to fall asleep, I asked Orin, "What'll I have to do now that I am the teacher's pet?"

"You'll have to do your best to rhyme and be poetic in order to keep that position. And let me tell you, when your buddies catch on, you'll have some real competition," he replied.

I lay there and jotted down the most poetic rhyming words that I could think of before I went to sleep.

Burley-Squirrelly
Stick-Quick
Pond-Fond

The list went on and on and just before I turned in for good, I rhymed one last time. "Good *night.* Sleep *tight.* Don't let the bed bugs *bite.*"

Orin just laughed.

24

As the Burley Cured

My, was Orin right!! He had told me that holding my position as teacher's pet was not going to be easy. I had wooed Miss Frances with my insightful rhyme and claimed my position. But on the second day of school, the real battle began.

Tal Smothers was the first to take a shot at my title. The day had started as usual, and then it happened. We had just finished saying the pledge, and Tal raised his hand.

"Yes, Tal. Do you have something to say?" Miss Frances recognized my nemesis.

"I wrote a little something last night that I would like to share with the class," he said, then glanced at me with a subtle grin. "It's not much. It is just two couplets."

"We'd be glad to hear it," Miss Frances replied with a look of surprise. "And oh, how good it is to hear someone using such great poetic terminology."

Tal stood next to his seat, pulled a wrinkled sheet of paper out of his pocket, cleared his throat, and began to read.

"As we pledge the flag of this great land;
Our heart is covered with our right hand.
We're free to speak and we're free to be;
What we want because of liberty."

Tal finished and looked up at Miss Frances to see what kind of reaction his "two cent" couplets had earned him. She was "speechless"—so she claimed. I was shocked that she enjoyed Tal's feeble attempt at poetry.

It was obvious on many of the students' faces that they too had discovered Miss Frances' weakness for poetry. I could sense a feeling of poetry anarchy brewing in the room. The battle was on.

The very next morning, little Brooks Melvin came armed with a Limerick to dethrone Tal.

"There once was a student at Roy G. Biv
Who had a strong desire to give,
His heart to poetry
And if you ask me,
That's a wonderful way to live."

I could tell Miss Frances was less impressed with the limerick than she'd been with Tal's rhymes and mine. I guess that it wasn't rich or deep enough to prove that Brooks put much thought into his work. It wasn't much, but he did have the throne for a day.

As much as I hated to do it, I was going to fight back. I liked my place at the top on the first day of school and I wanted it back. I wanted it back for good.

That night I went home and asked Gil for a book on poetry. I read a chapter about sonnets, elegies, and some other fancy styles, but the one that I knew would be simple and yet impressive was the haiku. Yeah, anybody could write three lines using the 5-7-5 pattern but I knew that with a little reading up on the history of the haiku, I would truly be inspired to write some doozies.

I read and found out that you were supposed to focus on nature while you wrote haikus, and that was to my advantage because I knew the outdoors like the back of my hand. I read the entire chapter on haiku, then started writing.

My first few were a little rocky but then words about nature seemed to flow like water onto my paper.

Burley Tobacco
14 L 8 Golden Leaf
Curing in the Barn

Of course I had to write one about fishin'.

Large mouth, or Small Mouth
Kentucky, Striped, All are Bass
Wonders in the Stream

I also wrote one about the mammoth ginseng root that Orin and I had dug.

Native Ginseng Plant
Years in the still woods alone
Valuable Root

I was a haiku writing machine until I finally dozed off after number ten.

I decided to save my haiku ammo until Monday so I could polish up a small research paragraph to include with my barrage.

Friday morning, Tal retaliated in pathetic manner against Brooks' limerick to regain one day as Miss Frances' pet. I don't even know what the poem was about, but he used enough rhyme to drive a person crazy.

On Monday morning, I made sure that I was the first person in the door. I laid a copy of the history of the haiku on Miss Frances' desk so that she would wonder, *Who took the time to research the haiku?* I had really thought this whole thing out.

No one saw me place it on her desk, and as soon as she came in I noticed that she did pause, read the small paragraph, and looked up with a grin. She announced, "There is someone who has really gone above the call of duty and completed some really good research on the haiku. Would our mystery poet please speak up?" I never dreamed she'd make such a performance out of the whole thing. But I guess when you want to be at the top, you'll go above and beyond in order to get there.

I raised my hand, stood, and declared to the class, "I did the research on the haiku, Miss Frances, and I even took the time to write ten of them just for fun."

Miss Frances put her hands over her heart and asked, "Can we hear a few of your haiku, Sean?"

Of course, my answer was yes and I proceeded to read not a couple but *all* of my haiku to the class. I could tell by the looks on my classmate's faces that I had proven myself worthy of being the teacher's pet for the remainder of the year. There were no more competitors for the crown from that day on. It is probably a good thing too, because my next set of ammunition was going to be a full-blown Shakespearian sonnet. I didn't want to go that far.

That evening I told Orin what I had done, and even he could not believe that I would go that far in order to be the teacher's pet. I let him read the haiku, and when he read the one about the ginseng root he spoke out.

"Sean, we need to check on our seng roots tonight," he said

"All of the roots should be dry enough to sell," I replied.

"We need to sell it so we can have a little money to spend," Orin stated with $ signs in his eyes.

When we stepped off the bus the air was filled with a strong smell. It was the smell of the tobacco curing in the barns. During this time of year, we always left the barn doors open so air would circulate throughout the barn and the leaves would dehydrate. Much of the lower and middle leaves had already turned brown but the tip leaves, which are always the last to cure, were still yellow and green. I had been so busy with my poetry war that I hadn't even noticed the tobacco curing. It wouldn't be long until we'd be stripping off the leaves and preparing to sell the crop.

Remembering that we had talked about looking at the seng roots when we got home, we went immediately to the laundry room where the roots had been left to dry. Mom knew the value of the roots so she never laid anything on them or even moved them, for that matter.

I carefully grabbed the towel and took it to the living room floor to examine the roots. Just like I had predicted, all of the roots were fully dried, even the mammoth, and they were ready to sell. We took the roots off the towel and put them in a saltine cracker box. The roots filled one box completely and about one fourth of another box. We used the saltine boxes because it was a general rule that one saltine box filled with seng roots roughly equaled one pound. It was an easy way to figure how much you had before you took it to Smothers' to sell.

We placed the mammoth root on the top of the other roots so that everyone would be sure to see it when we took it to sell. Despite the fact that it had been drying for several weeks, the root was still enormous. It had turned a bit yellow, which is normal for drying ginseng, and there were deep, visible wrinkles, which were also normal. It sure was beautiful.

"Let's ask Dad if he'll take us to Smothers' Saturday so that we can sell our seng," Orin stated.

"He's going to town anyway so we'll just ride along," I replied with $ signs in my eyes.

The rest of the evening, Orin and I talked about what we were going to spend our share of the money on. Orin actually had a list of things that he wanted. I just wanted a new pocketknife and a pair of work boots that were on sale at Smothers'.

That was the longest week ever. All we could do was wait until Saturday to sell our seng.

I simply performed my duties as Miss Frances' pet and waited patiently as the week was spent and the Burley cured.

25

Ginseng Heroes

When Saturday did finally decide to show up, Orin and me were both up at the crack of dawn just to make sure Dad didn't go to town without us. I double checked to make sure that we had picked up all of the seng roots and put them into the cracker boxes.

Dad came walking into the kitchen where we were getting our seng roots together and asked in a joking manner, "What are you boys gonna do with all of the money you're gonna make today?"

"I know that I'm gonna buy a new skinning knife and some boots," I replied.

Orin was still trying to figure out all that he might buy. After just a bowl of cereal, we headed for town.

The nights had really grown cold, and October was almost gone. Dad stopped by the barn down at Mr. Malone's to check and see how the tobacco was curing. Now almost all of the leaves had lost their color and the only parts that still needed to cure were the stems. There was only about three weeks until we'd be stripping the leaves from the tobacco. Dad propped open a door that had blown shut, and we proceeded down the road.

All of the now vacant tobacco fields that we passed were green with cover crop that had been sown in order to hold the soil. Next spring it would be plowed under. About the only crop left to be harvested was the field corn. Just like with the tobacco, a farmer had to wait until the ears of corn cured and lost most of the moisture it held before he could pick it.

We finally pulled up to Smothers' grocery, and we all hopped out of the truck. Orin carried the full box of seng roots, and I carried the partially filled box. As soon as we walked in, Mr. Smothers and some other folks who had been standing around talking, turned and looked at what we had brought.

"Well, it looks like the Merry boys have been busy," one fellow said.

Mr. Smothers replied, "And they kept a good secret because I don't remember being told about a seng patch big enough to render this much."

They all laughed.

"Let's weigh up, boys," Mr. Smothers said as he walked over to his scales.

Orin and I followed. Orin handed Mr. Smothers the full box of seng, and he dumped it out onto the scales.

We all watched the scales and Mr. Smothers said, "One pound, one and one half ounce."

We had been able to fit more than a pound in the box. While everyone was staring at the scales, I slipped the mammoth root out of my box and reached the box to Orin. Orin passed the box on to Mr. Smothers, and he dumped it onto the scales.

"Four ounces even." Mr. Smothers said. "Is that all you have to be weighed?" he went on to ask.

Orin looked at me, and I pulled the mammoth root from behind my back. All eyes were now peering at the root, and each one of the onlookers closed in for a closer look.

"Where in tarnation did you find such a seng root, boy?" an old gentleman asked, knowing I wouldn't tell.

"That is by far the biggest seng root I've ever seen," Mr. Smothers proclaimed. "Lay that thing on the scales," he demanded as he emptied what was already on there.

I laid the tangled mass of roots onto the scales and awaited the results. Mr. Smothers and all of the other old gents, including Dad, were crowded so close to the scales that Orin and me couldn't even see.

"I've never heard of such, but that root weighs one and three-quarter ounce," Mr. Smothers said as the crowd began to back away.

"Well, how much total did we have, and what is seng bringing this year?" Orin asked hurriedly.

"You boys brought in one pound, seven and one quarter ounces, and seng is bringing $275 dollars this year," he replied while punching in some numbers on his calculator. "That means you boys are $399.61 richer than you were when you came in the door," he went on to say.

I was speechless, and so was Orin. We gave each other a high five, then Orin disappeared into the rows of merchandise.

"If you boys don't care," Mr. Smothers began to speak, "I'd really like to make sure that this big root doesn't go to China but instead make sure that it stays right here in Kentucky. So I am going to keep it here in the store for everyone to see."

"That's fine by me," I replied.

"Me too," Orin echoed.

Mr. Smothers walked to the cash register and counted out our money.

"I'll just round that amount up to an even $400 so that it's easier for you boys to split," he said with a big smile.

"Thank you Mr. Smothers," I replied with a bigger smile.

He handed me the money, and I stood there in awe. I had never held so much money in all my life. Orin quickly came over and counted out his two hundred dollars.

While Orin and I shopped around the store, Mr. Smothers put the mammoth root in a box all to its self. He said that he was going to put it in a shadow box and hang on the wall. He even said that he was going to put our names on the box so everyone would know who had dug the root. I felt honored.

Before we left, I bought a new pair of boots and a small knife just perfect for skinning squirrels and rabbits. I also bought a handful of stick candy for Starr and Tempest. They had asked me to buy them something so I did what a good big brother should and bought them the candy. Orin bought a little radio, a spotlight so powerful that it'd burn a bullfrog's eyes out, a hat, and a set of tools. After we paid for the items, we got in the truck and started home.

I never felt so good about earning something in my whole life. I was already making plans for next year's seng season. I contemplated where I could find more patches like the one we found this past season. Not much was said on the ride home, but Dad did tell us that he was proud of us for working so hard to earn our own spending money. He went on to tell us how he had sold hazelnuts to earn some extra money when he was a boy. He also told us how that he had worked for a janitor at school when he was a boy, and the janitor paid him by giving him a .22 rifle. Dad still had the rifle, but I was unaware of where it had come from until then.

We pulled up to the house and Starr and Tempest ran out to meet us. I gave them the candy sticks, and they ran off to eat their sugary treats.

An unusually cool autumn chill filled the air, and we spent the rest of the day cutting and splitting firewood. Dad let Orin use the chainsaw for a while, which I thought was a bit scary, but he did quite well.

Dad did a great job not forcing new jobs on us. Instead he broke us in slowly. We cut wood until we made a fairly good-sized stack up at the barn. When we finally finished, we put the chainsaw in the tool room and checked the tobacco to see how well it was curing.

"These cool days and nights are really taking the moisture out of the stems now," Dad said as he looked at the tobacco.

"How long until we begin stripping?" Orin inquired.

"I'd say that it'd only be a couple weeks," he answered.

We walked to the house as the day came to a close. Both Orin and I put our money in a secret hiding place.

The next morning at church Orin and I were sure to give an offering at church as a way of thanking God for the sale of our seng roots. We were also bombarded with people inquiring where on earth we had found such a big seng root. Mr. Smothers had not wasted any time finding a shadow box to display the root, and we had become Ginseng heroes.

For the next several weeks we were greeted by young and old concerning the mammoth root. I felt like a celebrity. There was one old fella from a couple counties over that had been digging roots for seventy years, and he said that he'd never seen anything like the root on display at Smothers' store.

The buzz never seemed to wear off, but as fall became downright cold, there was a new stir in the air. Dad began visiting the barns more often to check the condition of the burley. We all knew that we'd be spending some long hours in the tobacco stripping room very soon. I tried not to think about it.

To occupy my mind in the evenings, and to insure that I didn't think about stripping tobacco, I wrote a poem. I called it, "The Ginseng Heroes."

I had become a lyrical genius.

And yes, I did share it with Miss Frances and the rest of the class. Of course, she loved it.

26

The Beginning of the End

There are some things about growing tobacco that you dread because the task is difficult or strenuous. What came next was neither, but I dreaded it sorely.

Stripping tobacco is one of the easiest tasks, physically, associated with growing tobacco. It was the mental strain that was unbearable. I mean, you could train a monkey to do the job, but it would literally "Go bananas."

Before we were able to sell the tobacco, we had to strip the leaves off from each stalk and separate them into three different grades. The leaves would be tied together and placed in a storage area that we called "the press" because we pressed the leaves down very tightly. After we finished stripping all of the tobacco we'd take the leaves to a market, where they would be sold.

As a young boy with tons of energy, the last thing on my list of likes was standing still. I loved to always be on the move, but when you stripped tobacco, you basically stood in one place for long periods of time.

Now that the air was getting colder as winter approached, we had seen some snow. Cold air seemed to be one of the requirements for stripping tobacco. The cold air wasn't only hard on the workers, but it made it hard to get the tobacco "In case."

What I mean by "In case" is "ready and able to strip." The tobacco could not be too moist or too dry when you stripped it. If it was too wet, then it would heat up in the press and rot. If you stripped it when it was too dry, it would crumble and it would be too light. The best days to catch the tobacco in case were the moist, rainy days.

On the first Friday of November, we had a warm spell and some rain moved into the area. This was our time to begin stripping. Orin and I stayed home from school that day to help Dad get the tobacco down from the barn and put it into a big heap called "a bulk."

Orin climbed into the barn and began dropping the tobacco, stick by stick, out onto the ground. Dad and I would go get the sticks of tobacco and pull the stalks off the stick. Dad made it look easy, but Billy Whittle's splintery sticks made it nearly impossible for me to remove the stalks.

We put the stalks into a nice neat pile and then we pressed it down. The bulk would get really large by the time we were finished. We did this because it helped to seal the moisture into the leaves. If we would have left the tobacco hanging, it would eventually dry out again.

Orin was really quick at dropping the tobacco down—so quick that a few times he dropped a stick of tobacco on me as I bent to pick up a stick. I was careful to watch out for him from there on.

Every ten minutes or so, I would gather up the sticks that had been cleaned off and put them into the tobacco stick pile. That way we wouldn't have to pick them up later.

We continued until we had bulked the entire lower shed of the barn, then covered the bulk with a large piece of black plastic.

"When are we going to start stripping?" I asked Dad.

"As soon as we get something to eat," he replied.

We made a meal out of bologna and potato chips. Then Dad, Orin, and I all carried an armload of wood back to the strip room. Dad started a fire in the old wood burning stove to keep out the chill.

Instead of stripping the tobacco that we had put into the bulk, we stripped the tobacco straight out of the barn. Orin dropped about 30 sticks of tobacco out of the barn, then we took the stalks off each stick and carried them into the strip room to begin.

Stripping tobacco was a lot like Henry Ford's assembly line that I had learned about last year in school. There was a large bench that you placed the tobacco on and the stripping began.

There were three basic grades of tobacco that we stripped off. If you want to get technical about it, there are more than three grades, but we only worried about Trash, Lugs, and Red.

Trash leaves, the bottom leaves, were called trash for a reason. They were the least attractive leaves on the plant. There were usually about 6-7 trash leaves on each plant. Orin stripped off the trash from the bottom of the stalks and passed the stalks to Dad.

Dad stripped off the lugs. The lugs were the longest leaves on the stalk and were a light auburn color. On most stalks, there were about 12-15 lug leaves. Dad stripped the lugs because he could tell where the lugs changed into red leaves and plus, he was a lot faster than Orin or me. After all the lugs were removed, Dad passed the stalk to me.

I stripped the remaining leaves from the stalk. The leaves on the tip were called "Red" leaves. There were usually 6 or 8 red leaves on each stalk and, of course, they were red. After I stripped all of the red leaves off, I pitched the bare stalk to the end of the bench. That process would continue, stalk by stalk, until all of the tobacco had been stripped.

After we accumulated a large pile of stalks, we'd take them out and put them onto a trailer hitched to Ole Red. There was nothing about the tobacco plant that went to waste. After we filled the trailer with stalks, Orin and I would take the stalks to the now empty tobacco fields and scatter them all over. They would be turned under next spring as compost.

After you stripped several stalks, you ended up with a handful of leaves. Dad always had to remind me how to tie the hands of tobacco together.

"You take two good leaves and wrap them about two times around the stems of the hand. Then you spread the leaves apart and bring the two leaves that you are wrapping with under the hand and pull it up," Dad would say as he demonstrated the technique.

It sounds harder than it really is. We would stack the hands of tobacco on the bench, which would later be taken out to the press to store.

"You know boys, there is talk that this may be the last year that the markets are going to take hand-tied tobacco," Dad said while holding a perfectly tied hand up to the light to examine it.

Orin turned and asked, "What will we do with the tobacco if they won't buy hand ties?"

"There's a new baling technique that the extension agent is supposed to demonstrate next spring at the extension office. They say that each farmer will need to make three boxes, one for each grade of tobacco, and you will actually bale the tobacco sort of like we do hay," he answered.

"Whoever heard of such!" I stated.

"It's supposed to be easier to handle and maybe a little quicker. We just have to get used to something new," Dad said assuredly.

"Easier and quicker sounds good to me," Orin said.

"I guess we'll find out next year," I commented.

The three of us exchanged a lot of thought and opinions for the rest of the evening. We stripped until about 5 o'clock that evening, then walked to the house to eat dinner. Hallie and Gillian had returned home from school and would come to help us strip after dinner. With them, we could get two crews going and get the job done quicker.

That evening truly was the beginning of the end of the tobacco season. Not to mention, it was also the beginning of the stripping room blues.

27

Stripping Room Blues

The Blues had set in. For the next several weeks, our evenings and Saturdays would be spent in the confines of our 12' x 20' strip room. We each marched to the barn, firewood in hand, like soldiers on a mission. In fact, I was on a mission. I was on a mission to get the burley stripped as quickly as possible.

On our first evening of stripping, we continued to strip straight from the barn. The damp air allowed the tobacco to stay in case all evening long. We'd save the tobacco in the bulk for tomorrow. With the girls now helping, we were able to do a lot more in less time.

At about 10:00 p.m. that night, Dad ended our shift and we went to the house. We knew the end of our day was drawing nigh because Dad hadn't put any wood onto the fire for quite some time. He allowed the fire to burn out so the barn wouldn't catch on fire. I noticed on my way out that the trailer attached to Ole Red was heaping full of tobacco stalks. That was a sure sign Orin and I would be scattering stalks first thing in the morning.

I was sure not to linger long at the barn, because I was in need of a shower. If I waited around, I'd have to wait until Orin finished with his shower and he stayed in there for an eternity.

I showered and went straight to bed. We had put in a long day, and I knew that many more just like it lay ahead.

The next morning Mom prepared a buffet of breakfast food. It was her way of pepping us up for a day of stripping burley. I ate biscuits and gravy with a side of pancakes that were conveniently shaped like tobacco leaves. We ate until we could eat no more because we knew there were few breaks to be taken until lunch.

We each grabbed a few sticks of wood to take to the strip room with us. Everyone but Orin, that is. Instead of carrying wood, he carried the new radio that he had bought with his seng money. I knew he didn't intend to listen to music because Dad wouldn't allow it. He said it took away from our family time. Instead, Orin planned to listen to the University of Kentucky Wildcats play basketball, which was approved by Dad. We loved to listen to the Wildcats play basketball. It was almost like we knew the players and we cheered them on each year from our dusty strip room. Tip off was not until noon, so we had plenty of time to prepare for the game. Gil and Hallie stayed behind for the time being. They helped Mom clean up the dishes and kitchen before they came up. This also allowed time for the strip room to warm up.

Dad lit a fire in the stove, and before we began pulling leaves, Orin and me had to take the load of stalks out to the field and scatter them. This was another time that I was allowed to drive Ole Red because you had to drive relatively slow to avoid dumping the entire load. I drove the load nice and slow to the field, and Orin rode on the trailer. As I entered the field, he began to toss the stalks overboard. We made sure we scattered the stalks well because Dad didn't like it when we scattered them too thickly because it made plowing extra challenging the next spring. After we emptied the load, we returned to the barn where we'd fill the trailer many more times before the stripping was over.

Upon returning, Orin brought in a couple armloads of burley from the bulk. By now, Gil and Hallie had finished helping Mom clean up the kitchen and had arrived. In order for us to make the assembly line work with five people, we simply started in the middle and since Orin could strip the trash leaves off the stalks quickly, he could toss the stalks either direction. Dad stripped lugs on one side, and Gillian stripped lugs on the other. Hallie stripped the red on one end of the table, and I stripped the red off on the other. It worked slick as a whistle, as Uncle Carve would say.

Armload after armload, we whittled away at the bulk. The bulk was so big that it took quite a while to notice we had actually stripped some off from it. I had mastered the technique of tying the hand of tobacco together by midmorning. By then we were also accumulating several hands of tobacco in the press. We kept all of the tied hands in a press in order to seal in the moisture.

At about 10:30, Mom and the twins showed up at the strip room. The twins were following Mom, who was carrying a basket with our lunches in it. Mom relieved me of my duties so I could play with Star and Tempest.

At first we played under the strip bench, but the strip room was so drafty we soon decided it was a bit too cool to play down there. We then went to the corner nearest the stove and took broken pieces of sheetrock and wrote our names on the wall. Well, I wrote my name, and the twins just scribbled. They were a little young to be writing anything that made sense. I drew several pictures on-demand. I drew Ole Red, Smif, and the entire Merry family. The twins laughed when I finished the family portrait, because I had drawn Orin with an oversized and distorted head. Orin didn't think it was funny.

At about 11:30, Dad turned on the radio, adjusted the antennae, and found a station that was airing the pre-game show. "The UK Wildcats are taking on the Volunteers of Tennessee," the radio announcer stated.

"This ought to be a good game," Dad said as he made one final adjustment to the antennae.

At high noon the game began, and there was actually very little said within the strip room. There was an occasional "Oooh" or "Ahh" as the announcers excitedly relayed the highlights to us. There were times when I could see the game being played out inside my mind. I had never been to the famous Rupp Arena, but I had an imagination large enough to imagine it. At half time Orin and I made another trip to the field to empty another load of stalks. We scattered the stalks as quickly as possible so we wouldn't miss one second of the basketball action.

The Wildcats went on to win the game that day by a narrow margin. They also managed to take our minds off the menial task of stripping tobacco for a few hours. We never really paid attention to the job but instead to the game, and by the end of the game we noticed that we had stripped enough tobacco to fill the trailer with stalks again. The big bulk we had started with early that morning had shrunk to half its original size.

After the post-game show, we had a late lunch. "Today's special is your choice of a turkey, ham, or bologna sandwich along with a lunch cake and a can of pop to wash it down with," Mom joked as she passed out our food.

As soon as we finished eating, we resumed stripping the tobacco. Mom took the twins back to the house because it was time for their afternoon nap. Sometimes, when there was just one crew stripping, Mom would make the twins a bed out of jackets on the strip bench and they'd sleep while we worked. But this time, since every inch of the strip bench was being used, she had no choice but to take them to the house.

At about 6 o'clock that evening, we had finished stripping the bulk of tobacco. It was a major accomplishment, but there was a lot more to do before we could say we were totally finished for the season.

Day after day and evening after evening, except for Sundays, of course, we stripped burley. Ten days after we started stripping the tobacco, we had emptied the barn on our farm. Dad had called to reserve a spot for our crop, and he took the tobacco to the tobacco warehouse in Maysville where it would be stored until November 28th. Dad made arrangements for all of our tobacco to be sold on the 28th. Now we just had to strip all of the burley that was still hanging in Mr. Malone's barn.

It was a few days until the burley season would be over, but until then, we'd suffer through what was left of the stripping room blues.

28

To Market, To Market…

Five wins and two losses into the UK basketball season, we were able to proclaim that our stripping room blues could come to an end. Each year it seemed like such a burden had been lifted when we finished. All we had to do now was take the last load of tobacco to the warehouse to be stored until our November 28th sale date. Dad had taken a load to the warehouse earlier in the week.

The night before we took the tobacco to Maysville, Dad, Orin, and I loaded the hands of tobacco into the back of the truck. Dad stayed in the back of the truck and Orin and I packed the hands to Dad. Dad was able to press the hands of burley down so we could fit more onto the truck. When we finished loading the last hands, we covered the load with a tarpaulin in order seal in the moisture. Orin and I looked forward to the trip to market each year.

The three of us got up extra early the next morning, so that we could get to the warehouse before the rush of other farmers. I never ate anything before we left because I had a history of getting carsick. We were off to market, to market, but not to buy a fat pig.

Dad had to start the truck early in order to thaw the frost-covered windshield. As we approached the truck, we could see our breath. Orin always got to sit nearest the door and I sat in the middle. After we buckled our seatbelts, to market we went.

The road to Maysville was the curviest road that had ever been constructed. At least that is what Uncle Carve always said. All along the way we watched for an occasional deer or other form of wildlife in the fields we passed. The only real color in all of the valleys we drove through was the green of the cover crop growing on the now-barren tobacco fields. We passed several farms where they were loading tobacco onto their trucks in order to take to market. Dad knew how to beat the rush.

The entire trip took about two and one half hours, but it seemed much longer. Dad entertained us by listening to AM radio news. I never could understand the announcer because of the static, but Dad listened as if every word was crystal clear. When the station faded to the point that even Dad could not understand it, Dad chimed in.

"You boys see that farm over there?" he asked.

We nodded.

"I helped build each one of those barns when I first started building," he continued.

Dad pointed to various structures and farms, telling us about his years as a builder.

When we finally reached the city of Maysville, the fog was thick enough to cut. Dad crept his way through the sleepy little streets and made the last turn into Sharp's Tobacco Warehouse. There were several other warehouses such as Moyer's, Tiller's, Boxer, and Globe just to name a few. Each year I asked Dad the same question.

"Dad, why do we always come to Sharp's Warehouse and not any of the others?" I asked.

"Sean, I've always come to Sharp's because they really treat the farmer right," Dad began his reply. "I have seen Mr. Sharp argue and really take up for us when he felt that the buyers were not treating us fairly by paying low prices."

Dad finished his reply as we drove into the warehouse. The warehouse was enormous. It was definitely the biggest building that I had ever been in. There were already three truckloads of tobacco in front of us waiting to be unloaded. We pulled up behind the third truck.

An army of men worked like busy little ants. They were taking the tobacco off the trucks and placing the hands on tobacco baskets. They really knew what they were doing. The way they stacked the hands made such a neat circular design—sort of like a big flower. Since so many men were helping unload, it didn't take long for them to begin unloading our truck.

"Hello there, Mr. Sharp," Dad shouted across the way.

"Well, how is the Merry family?" Mr. Sharp was a tall skinny man who squinted his eyes and looked over his glasses as he talked to you. He approached Dad, and they shook hands. "So does this finish you up for the year?" Mr. Sharp inquired.

"Yeah, this is the last of our crop," Dad replied.

"How did it weigh? Do you think you'll have your quota?" Mr. Sharp inquired further.

"Oh, I think we'll have plenty. We should have some left over," Dad answered.

"I'm anticipating a lot of big buyers on the 28th, so things should go well," Mr. Sharp said with confidence.

"I certainly hope so," Dad began. "Our old tractor is about to give out on us, and I was hoping to use some of this year's money to make a downpayment on another."

"You know I'll do all that I can," Mr. Sharp assured Dad.

"Thank you," Dad said as he again shook Mr. Sharp's hand.

Mr. Sharp turned and began to walk away. He stopped and shouted to Dad, "Arden, you be sure to send the boys down to my office. I've got something for them."

Orin and I always looked forward to going to the warehouse because Mr. Sharp always had some goodies for the kids.

As the men continued to unload our truck, Orin and I made our way to Mr. Sharp's office. We ran back and forth between the many support posts in the warehouse. We were careful not to run out in front of one of the many forklifts carrying baskets of tobacco all around. We hid behind the baskets of tobacco. The cured burley left a sweet smell in the air. After a few minutes of hiding just for fun, we raced to Mr.

Sharp's office. Orin won, of course, but I was really getting faster. I knew it wouldn't be long until I would keep up with him.

As we entered Mr. Sharp's office, he squinted up over his glasses. "Come on in, boys. I have a little something for you." He reached into his drawer and pulled out a box. "There was a fella who came here selling these things, and I told him I knew a couple boys that needed one," he said as he opened the box.

Orin and I both looked into the box. There, before our eyes, was a selection of new pocketknives. My heart was about to beat out of my chest with excitement.

"Take your time and choose one that you like," he said with a smile.

We went over to a dusty old couch and began looking at the knives. I chose a short lock blade that had an imitation pearl handle. I thought it would be good and sturdy to dig seng with. Orin chose a long slender knife that I knew he'd use to skin squirrels.

"Thank you so much, Mr. Sharp," Orin said as he handed the box of knives back.

"Yes, thank you," I followed.

"You boys are certainly welcome. You just be careful and don't get hurt," he replied with a squinty smile.

We turned and left the office. If being happy meant that you were on cloud nine, then Orin and I were on cloud twenty. We never really said much as we walked back toward the truck. Our eyes were fixed on our new knives. We swapped back and forth, looking at what the other had chosen.

When we reached the truck, Dad was handing off the last bit of tobacco. "Looks like you boys got a little treat. Did you get me one?" Dad asked jokingly.

We each handed our knives to Dad. He looked at them and just smiled. He was happy for us.

Dad then walked over to a little booth and they wrote him out a ticket telling how many pounds he had brought. It was also a custom of the warehouses to give the farmer a check that was called a "haul bill." The amount of the haul bill was based on how much tobacco you brought and was meant to help the farmer pay for the hauling expenses.

Dad said his good-byes, and we got in the truck to begin our journey home. By then there were at least ten trucks waiting to be unloaded.

The ride home never seemed to take as long as the trip there. Along the way we stopped at a little gas station and got a pop and a sandwich. I got a roast beef sandwich just because it was never offered on our menu at home.

The remainder of the ride home was pretty much the same as the ride there, only there were new thoughts crossing each of our minds. Orin and I were both still daydreaming about what we were going to do with our new knives while Dad contemplated how well this year's sale would go. Only time would tell.

Home again, Home again. Jiggity jig.

29

A Day of Thanks

For many families Thanksgiving was one of the few days that the whole family actually ate together and the head of each home would ask a blessing on the food. It was certainly a special day to us but Dad always prayed, no matter the day, and we always ate together, no matter the day.

Mom was planning to fix a few extra helpings of each dish because Billy Whittle and his Mrs. were planning to eat with us. Both Billy and Blenda had family, but they lived too far away to make a quick visit. So we made plans to have them over.

We never had school the day before or the day after Thanksgiving so Orin, Dad, and I had time to do some rabbit hunting. It had become sort of a tradition for us to make a serious rabbit hunt early each Thanksgiving Day.

By the time we got ready to go hunting, Mom had already been up mixing and blending her gourmet meal. Even Gil and Hallie were helping Mom. They tried to complete as much as possible before Starr and Tempest awoke and demanded to help.

Dad came out of his room with his 12 gauge and my .410. Orin was carrying his 20 gauge. Dad had a system that we had to graduate through. It progressed as we got older and it allowed us to use bigger guns as we hunted. Everybody had to start with the single shot .410. After you learned to handle it and use it properly, you graduated to the 20 gauge. Then after you proved yourself with the 20 gauge, you graduated to the 12 gauge. Dad was very serious about the way that we handled guns when we hunted, and we knew hunting was no time to be joking around.

We each ate a bowl of cereal and made our way to the door. I put on my hunting vest and followed Dad and Orin out the back door. Just as we were leaving, Mom reminded Dad, "Don't forget that Billy and Blenda will be here about 12:30 and we are going to eat at 1:00."

"Don't worry. We'll be back in plenty of time," Dad assured Mom.

As we stepped outside, the cold air greeted us along with Smif. He knew what the shiny instruments in our hands were, and he knew what we intended to do with them. He jumped and barked with excitement.

"Are you ready to jump up some cotton tails, ole boy?" I asked Smif in a tantalizing manner. He barked his reply even harder.

We made our way across the gravel road in front of our house and entered a weedy field where there were always plenty of rabbits. Dad stopped and put shells in his gun. Orin and I knew it was time for us to do the same thing. I pulled a slender .410 shell from my pocket, broke down the gun, slid the shell into the chamber, and closed the chamber. I had a bit of a disadvantage to Dad and Orin because I only had one shell in my gun. They each had three shells in their guns. I also had to be closer to the rabbit because my gun was smaller than and not as powerful as theirs. But I had to start somewhere.

Smif had already jumped into the weeds and was sniffing a cold trail.

"You boys watch that brush pile. Smif usually stirs a rabbit out of there," Dad suggested.

Dad had barely finished his sentence when Smif let out his first bark. It was a quick, high-pitched bark. That was a sign the rabbit's trail was getting a little warmer. Shortly, Smif broke out into a series of long, sad barks that signaled he was closing in on the rabbit. Suddenly, the weeds shook, and a big rabbit darted out of the brush pile Dad had referred to earlier.

"It's up, boys!!" Dad said excitedly.

Smif was in hot pursuit. The rabbit zigged and zagged and ole Smif followed with his nose to the ground. He was now using his famous "the rabbit's up" bark. It sounded like a continuous wail of happiness.

Dad was now walking toward the end of the field where he thought the rabbit would go. Orin and I followed. Dad told Orin to go across the creek where there were several rabbit holes. Orin would be able to get the rabbit if it tried to go in the hole. I had to stay near Dad.

"You need to watch way out in front of Smif," Dad told me.

"I see the rabbit!!" I nearly shouted.

"Shhh! Not so loud. Just wait until the rabbit passes those maple trees, and then it should be close enough to shoot," Dad instructed.

I waited and my heart raced like a thoroughbred. I raised my .410 and pulled back the hammer. It was hard to hold the gun steady because my heart was racing so fast. The rabbit hopped closer and closer, and I got more and more nervous. Finally, the rabbit reached the maple trees but instead of passing them, it hid behind them.

I had to wait longer, but finally, the rabbit hopped out from behind the tree. I squeezed the trigger. *BANG* went the gun, and I shot completely over the top of the rabbit. A branch of the maple tree got the worst end of the deal. The rabbit was now hightailing toward Orin. I was busy trying to reload my gun. Dad could have easily killed the rabbit, but he was letting us have our turn.

With a single shot from the 20 gauge, Orin was the first to get a rabbit. After Smif tracked his way to the rabbit, Orin petted his head, then Smif darted toward another weed patch, ready for more action.

It wasn't long until Smif notified us that he was on a cold trail. All we had to do was wait. Smif was working hard. I watched closely, then saw a bit of movement in the weeds in front of Smif.

"Dad, I see a rabbit," I said while pointing.

"Don't point with your finger! Point with your gun," Dad coached.

I raised my gun, pulled back the hammer, and this time I didn't miss. The rabbit was about 50 feet from Smif so it didn't take him long to catch up to it. I made my way over to my rabbit and held it up for Dad to see.

"That's the way to use that .410, Sean!" Dad cheered.

The morning hours passed much too quickly. By 11 o'clock we had each killed one rabbit. Dad suggested we get back home so we could clean the rabbits before our dinner guests arrived.

When we got home, Orin and I had our first opportunity to try out our new knives that Mr. Sharp had given us. Dad stood by and coached us as we cleaned the rabbits. He was a veteran rabbit skinner; we couldn't have asked for a better teacher. I was a little slower than Orin, but I did get my rabbit skinned to Dad's specifications. Orin skinned his and Dad's rabbits. Then we took the rabbits inside to be washed and put into the freezer.

When we went in, we each told our story of how we got our rabbit. The girls were grossed out, not impressed.

"You guys need to get cleaned up. Billy and Blenda just arrived," Mom insisted.

We went to the bathroom and took turns washing our hands. Nobody really dressed up for the Thanksgiving meal. We just cleaned up and put on decent clothes.

By the time I made it back into the living room, Orin was telling the Whittles how he'd killed his rabbit. He stressed the fact that he killed it with a single shot and that I had missed it. He forgot to mention that he missed two other rabbits later on, but that was typical for Orin.

The girls finished setting the table and we made our way to the dining room. I still don't know how Mom managed to cook so much food and not burn a single dish. When Blenda commented on the spread, Mom invited her over for some cooking lessons. "You'll never learn if you don't try," Mom told Blenda.

When we were seated, Dad said, "Let's give thanks to the Lord for all He has done."

We bowed our heads and Dad prayed. He thanked the Lord for loving us and giving Himself for us. He also thanked God for our family and friends and all of the blessings He gives us each day. Dad closed his prayer by asking God to bless the food and give us many happy years together. He ended with an "Amen" that was echoed around the table.

There was no need for a rush because Mom had fixed enough to feed us for several days to come. There was a big turkey with stuffing, mashed potatoes, green beans, corn, sweet potatoes, rolls, and of course, cranberry sauce.

I ate a little bit of everything. I even ate a second helping of cranberry sauce. It was the only time of the year when we got to eat it, so I indulged myself. Orin made weird shapes with his cranberry sauce. He was always doing weird things.

Dad dug out the wishbone from the turkey and handed it to Gil. She and Hallie got to pull it because they were the oldest. Orin and I always got to pull the wishbone when we ate chicken. Starr and Tempest would just have to wait.

The girls pulled, and Hallie ended up with the larger piece, which supposedly meant she'd get married first. She was flattered. I was annoyed by all of their mushy, gushy love stuff.

When we had finished the main course, Hallie and Gil brought in two fresh pumpkin pies for us to enjoy.

"The girls made these pies," Mom said proudly.

"In that case, I'll pass," Orin joked. Every female in the room gave him the evil eye. "I'm just joking," he quickly recanted.

Despite the jokes, the pie was really good. I piled mine high with whipped cream.

Shortly after the last piece of pie had been served, the men retired to the living room, and Dad and Billy reminisced of days gone by. The women did whatever women do in a kitchen full of leftovers.

That day I realized that, of all the families in the world, I was born into a special one. My heart was filled with thanks even if Orin was my brother.

The afternoon passed slowly as everyone talked and enjoyed themselves. Billy and Blenda left at about 4:00 with a week's supply of leftovers, which thrilled me to the core. I never was much on leftovers.

30

Auction Ears

The Monday following Thanksgiving was the day that our tobacco was to sell. Ever since we'd dropped off our burley at the market, the buzz at Smothers', Gracie Brothers, and everywhere else that people gathered was, "I wonder what the burley will sell for this year?" Dad always quoted the price from the year before. The tobacco had averaged $1.47 per pound last year, and we were always hopeful for a few cents more on the pound each year. Every penny helped.

The Sunday before the big sale, Brother Force preached a powerful sermon about Ananias and Saphira and how they had cheated God out of some money that they were supposed to give as an offering. As the story goes, the couple dropped dead and was buried the same day because of their sin. To end his message, Brother Force looked over his glasses at the congregation and reminded everyone, "God will get what is His." He was in no way soliciting funds. He was just reminding every farmer of where all blessings come from. Dad was a faithful giver, as well as the other farmers, and the church had been saving so we could make some much needed repairs to our aging church building.

That day after church, we had yet another great meal consisting of Thanksgiving leftovers. There was still some turkey left, mostly dark meat, some mashed potatoes, and lots of other goodies to choose from. Everyone except Mom was stuffing themselves as full as possible. It wasn't because the food was irresistible. We all knew the sooner we got rid of all the leftovers, the sooner Mom would cook fresh meals again.

After eating the scrumptious leftovers, I fell victim to the tryptophan in the turkey and fell asleep. The weather outside was nasty so I was able to fall asleep with a clear conscience that I wasn't wasting a good day. I slept until it was time to go to the evening church service.

Brother Force spoke for only a short time about the blessings of hard work. I know that every farmer, including Dad, was hoping for blessings when it came time for the buyers to purchase their crops tomorrow. Only a farmer could understand the true importance of this one crop, tobacco, to the existence of life itself.

When Brother Force dismissed the service he greeted everyone at the door as usual. As he and Dad shook hands, Brother Force said, "I know how much this crop means to you. The Lord will provide."

"I know He will, Brother Force. He has never let us down," Dad replied.

We all went to bed early that night because the warehouse was always extra crowded on sale day so we had to leave bright and early.

Long before the sun crept over the hilltops, Mom was waking her brood. It was a school day, but this was yet another time we were permitted to miss school. Tobacco had been a major part of everyone's life for so long, it was important that we know the ways of the market.

As usual before a long road trip, I ate very little. I would make up for it later at the little café inside the warehouse. Dad always let us eat a meal there on sale day. We drove the family car, one that was well used. I got to sit up front because it helped to minimize my vomiting reflexes. At least that's what I claimed.

The ride was eternal, but at the end of it was a year's pay.

I fell asleep somewhere along the way and awoke as we pulled into a bumpy parking lot at the end of the warehouse. We were finally there, and so were hundreds of other farmers. We were all there for the same reason.

There was a certain expression in the eyes of each farmer—a look of weary wonder. Each family had spent many field days in order to make ends meet.

We went inside the dimly lit warehouse and began to look for our crop. There were thousands of baskets of tobacco waiting to be auctioned to the buyers. To an untrained eye, all of the tobacco might look alike, but these buyers were critical and wanted the most for their money.

We walked aisle after aisle, turning over tags, looking for our name. Finally, in the third row, Gil found the tags that said, *Arden Merry.* We looked at the baskets of hand-tied burley, knowing it could possibly be the last year hand ties would be accepted. The baskets were perfect and beautiful. Rumor had it that next year farmers would be required to bale their tobacco. Mom had brought her camera so she could take our picture in front of the baskets as sort of a memorial to the days of hand-tied tobacco. We lifted Starr and Tempest up and allowed them to sit on top of the basket. Mom snapped several pictures.

After I recovered from the brightness of the flash, I noticed that many farmers were now searching for their crops as well. Dad had already engaged into a debate about how well he thought the sale would go. It was freezing cold inside the warehouse, but the talk was hot. Dad shared with everyone the news that he heard about the support price being $1.50. We could only hope. The support price was the bottom price that was set each year by the federal government. It guaranteed that farmers would get a fair price.

Everybody kept looking at their watches. We all knew the buyers wouldn't emerge from the nice, warm office until the minute the sale was to begin. Ten o'clock was the magic hour.

Finally, the time had come. The door to Mr. Sharp's office opened and about ten buyers, an auctioneer, and Mr. Sharp emerged. There were also a few men following who would be marking the price and tagging the baskets. They walked toward the place where they intended to start. All eyes were on these men. Dad seemed nervous. He and Mom each held one of the twins as we waited.

The auctioneer was the first man in the line. The buyers would split up. There would be half on one side of the baskets and half on the other. Mr. Sharp moved from side to side talking to the buyers and prodding them to pay top-dollar. The men marking and tagging the baskets followed.

Now the moment we had all been waiting for came. The auctioneer picked up a handful of tobacco from the first basket and began uttering words that sounded Greek to me.

"Gimmeonehalfonehalfonehalfonehalfanybodyonehalf," went the auctioneer.

Finally, the hand of a cautious buyer went up and now, so could the price. The procession continued slowly down the first row.

"I can't understand what he's saying, Dad," I said sincerely.

"Did you bring your ears?" Dad asked me in reply.

"Of course," I said while pointing to my ears.

"Oh no, Sean, those ears won't do. You needed to bring your Auction Ears," Dad said while laughing.

I laughed as well.

The procession continued and we made our way over to the first row to see what price was written on the tags. The first basket had nice long lug leaves. I picked up the tag. It had $1.52 written sloppily across it. Not a word was spoken. We only smiled and moved on to the next basket, which was piled high with hands of dark red leaves. I turned the tag over to find $1.53 scribbled on it.

"I had heard that they were going to pay top dollar for good red," Dad commented.

The trash leaves on the next basket sold for $1.50 per pound. Dad seemed pleased.

The procession continued to snake its way down the first row and back up the second. Once in a while you could hear Mr. Sharp heckling the buyers. He wanted them to pay the most for every farmer. Since our tobacco was in the third row, we would be next. We found a place near our baskets and waited. Soon the auctioneer picked up leaves from our first basket and began his jibber jabber.

We all watched and listened. Basket after basket, the buyers cast their bid. I thought I could pick out a few $1.53 bids, and I even thought I heard a $1.55 bid.

After the buyers and markers had passed our entire crop, our whole family made its way to the baskets to check the tags. I walked down the row and called out the prices.

"$1.52, $1.52, $1.53, $1.50, $1.50, $1.53," I continued. "Whoa, Dad, look at this!" I shouted. I had made it to the baskets of dark red leaves that were at the end of our crop. I held up a tag that said $1.55. There were two other baskets with the same price marked on them.

"Mr. Sharp always does me right," Dad said as he put his arm around Mom.

On and on went the auction until every basket had been sold in half of the warehouse. Another sale would follow in the afternoon. Now we would wait for our checks to be made out. Sometimes it took quite a while for the checks to be ready. It was now time to eat our annual meal in Sharp's café.

Sharp's café was a crude but good place to eat. As we entered the greasy air of the café, I knew what I would order. I always got a Sharp burger, onion rings, and hot chocolate. I needed all that I could get to warm me up. I could tell that Dad was really pleased with the way the sale had gone by the way he ordered his food. There had been a couple of years that the crops were not as good as usual and neither were the selling prices. On those occasions Dad would settle for just a Sharp burger and a coffee. This time Dad ordered the Super Sharp Steak Meal. It was a rather pricey item, but Dad deserved it.

Before the food arrived, Dad thanked God for the good sale. When our food did arrive we sat in the little booths and ate our greasy meals. I took my time and savored every bite. To me, there was no burger like a Sharp burger. The clanging of dishes and the sizzling of frying burgers filled the air.

"Do you think we made enough to fix Ole Red or get another tractor?" Orin asked with a mouthful.

"I'll have to pay all of my credits and bills and find out," Dad replied as he cut into his steak.

The remainder of the conversation revolved around the topic of tractors.

After we finished, Dad, Orin, and I went to the office to wait in line for our checks. All of the females were waiting in line to go to the restroom. One by one the receptionist called out a farmer's name.

"Arden Merry," the receptionist called out. We walked to the window. "Mr. Sharp would like to speak with you, Mr. Merry," the receptionist said as she pointed toward the door that led to Mr. Sharp's office.

As Dad opened the door, Mr. Sharp spun around in his chair and looked over his glasses. "Come on in, Merry men." He was always witty.

"So how did you think the sale went, Arden?" Mr. Sharp inquired.

"Things seemed to go really great, Mr. Sharp," Dad replied. "I'm certainly thankful for an abundance of dark red leaves this season."

"You never know what those buyers will want, but you certainly had it this year," Mr. Sharp said.

"Will the prices change much next year since everybody has to bale their crops?" Dad asked.

"Only time will tell...but I do know one thing," Mr. Sharp said with a slight pause. "You'll be pleased with your checks for this year."

Mr. Sharp handed Dad two checks. One was for the crop we had grown on our farm, and the other was for the crop from Mr. Malone's farm. Although Dad never did show us the sum of the checks, we assumed that the numbers were satisfactory based on Dad's smile as he took the checks from Mr. Sharp's outstretched hand. After a short conversation about the new baling regulations, we said our good-byes and began walking to the car where the rest of the clan was supposed to be waiting. As we walked toward the car Dad pointed to a large crowd on the far side of the warehouse.

"They are about to begin the second sale of the day," Dad explained.

"I sure hope they brought their Auction Ears," I said with a laugh.

The three of us laughed and walked away from a tradition that would be forever changed within the next year. I looked back one last time at the thousands of baskets of hand-tied burley. It was like saying good-bye to an old friend. I turned and continued toward the car.

The auctioneer's voice was now echoing in the distance.

31

Home Again, Home Again…

After leaving the icy tobacco warehouse, I didn't feel my toes until we were nearly home. Despite my efforts to weatherize my shoes, three pairs of socks still didn't keep my toes from nearly freezing off. Dad drove noticeably slower on the way home and appeared to be deep in thought most of the way. As we neared the entrance to Gracie Brothers, Dad turned on the blinker and pulled into the lot.

"I'll be back in just a moment," Dad said as he got out of the car.

Only Dad went in. Everyone was wondering what it was that Dad was doing. Was he going to order a new tractor? Was he just getting parts for Ole Red?

We watched Dad through the dirty picture window of the store. First, he walked toward the back of the store and picked up and examined some parts that were on a shelf. After he placed the parts back on the shelf he made his way to the front of the store, where he was greeted by the Gracie Brothers themselves.

The Gracie Brothers were an odd pair. They were twins, but it was obvious they weren't identical. They were as different as daylight and dark. I never knew their real names. Everyone just called one "Big" and the other "Little." It was not uncommon to hear people saying things like, "Big Gracie bought another farm down the road," or "Little Gracie's wife is expecting another child."

Big Gracie was exactly what you imagine. He was BIG! I'm no expert, but I'd say that when Big and Little Gracie were in the womb, Big Gracie hogged most of the nutrients. He was at least six feet ten inches tall and as broad as a barn door. I saw him sit down at a community dinner once, and he ate so much that it took Little and two others to get him back on his feet. I always wondered where he got clothes that fit him.

Little Gracie, on the other hand—it was no question where he got his clothes. One time Mom took me to get some new pants because I'd outgrown my hand-me-downs and, much to my surprise, Little Gracie was looking at pants on the same rack as me. Folks in town never tried to take advantage or make fun of Little because of his size, though. It was no secret he had a temper and strength the size of Jupiter.

Both Little and Big shook hands with Dad, then they commenced to speaking. We could only guess what they were discussing. The conversation seemed eternal, but Dad finally emerged from the store with a couple of papers in his hand and a semi-smile on his face. As he stepped out onto the sidewalk he paused, looked up, and seemed to stare at the sky. Then, he came on to the car. As he got in, he said, "Feels like there is gonna be a change out there."

We didn't know if Dad was being literal and speaking about the weather or if he was throwing us a curveball, meaning that things were gonna change around the Merry farm. The more I pondered, the more convinced I was that Dad was talking about the weather. The air outside was noticeably cold and damp. The clouds were thick as sheep's wool, and the wind was sharp as a knife. Maybe there was change in the air. Only time would tell.

I was never so happy to get home than I was on that day. Listening to Gil and Hallie argue and the nonsensical songs that Starr and Tempest sang were enough to annoy even the toughest.

As we stepped out of the car, Dad once again looked to the heavens and studied the overcast sky. "Yep. Change is in the air."

It was late evening when we got home and, since the winter daylight hours are so short, it was almost dark. We had to go back to school the next day, so everybody but Dad retired to bed early.

Dad stayed in the kitchen at the table with papers strewn everywhere. He was getting ready to settle all of his annual debts. Dad was an honest man, and he made sure everything he borrowed was paid back. One thing was certain. Dad would give the Lord what was His.

Before I went to bed, I walked to the kitchen to tell Dad good night and noticed the papers the Gracie Brothers had given him were in the midst of the pile. I went to bed wondering what was on the papers. Only time would tell.

I fell asleep wondering what Dad had meant by saying, "There is change in the air."

32

A Flaky Family

On most school nights it seemed as if the night hours zipped by in fast-forward. An eight-hour night seemed more like the blink of an eye. This night was a bit different. I slept for what seemed an eternity before I finally awoke from my slumber. I felt refreshed and ready to go, but something was strange. I never woke up on my own on a school day. Mom always had to wake me up. I began to wonder if I was dreaming. One glance at Orin, and I was convinced that I was not dreaming. I raised up and sat on the edge of the bed and listened. I could only hear some shuffling in the kitchen, but all else was quiet. I slid out of bed and crept into the kitchen, where I found Mom cooking.

"Mom, what time is it?" I inquired.

"Eight-thirty," she replied with her back still to me.

"8:30!! Mom, we had school today!" I said in surprise.

"Loretti would need a snow plow on the front of the bus to get you kids today," Mom said with a smile.

"Huh," I replied, confused, then peered out the window.

Sure enough Dad knew what he was talking about when he said there was change in the air. We had heard the weather men talking for a week about a large amount of moisture that was on its way, but I never dreamed it would come in frozen form. Sure, winter was drawing near, but this was too good to be true. The ground was covered in glorious school-canceling snow.

"How much is out there?" I asked.

"Your dad measured it this morning at 6:00, and there was already eight inches."

“Eight inches! It’s still snowing, too! No telling how much we’ll get!” I shouted.

“Your dad is already making provisions for you all to have plenty of snow tubes to use,” Mom said.

Deep inside I knew that this snow was catastrophic to those having to go to work in the corporate world, but it was sacred to the unincorporated world of my childhood. My shouting had been enough to raise the rest of the Merry clan to the surprise snow. We all looked out the window in awe.

The tobacco fields were beautifully blanketed in a pure white snow as smooth as silk.

“What are we waiting on? Let’s get out there and enjoy it!” Orin exclaimed.

Before embarking on our journey of joy, we had to consult the one master who had seemingly created the art of staying warm, Mom.

You see, when winter rolled around, we didn’t get new snowsuits filled with cotton and down feathers. Instead, we went to our closet and Dad’s closet to create what I liked to call the “Three-layer special.” Exquisitely designed by Mom, the three-layer special consisted of three layers of work clothes arranged from the tightest inside to the loosest on the outside. Once we were bundled up appropriately and approved by the authority, off we went.

We slowly trudged through the white wonder toward the barn, where Dad’s tracks were leading. The snow was still pouring from the heavens. Orin and I were trying to catch snowflakes on our tongue as we walked. I’m sure we looked ridiculous. When we reached the barn, we entered only to see Dad holding the inflated wonders that he had acquired at work. They were rubbish and junk to the outside world, but they were unmatched joy for us.

Each inner tube looked like a patchwork quilt with its many patches in place to stop the air from leaking out. After they passed Dad’s inspection, the tubes were handed over, and Orin and I journeyed on. To the top of the hill we slipped and slid. Finally, we reached the summit of Merry Mountain. It really wasn’t a mountain but from the top, the barns and the house looked small in comparison to our expectations of joy.

We were both out of breath, so we sat down on the tubes to rest before we began our descent.

"Can you believe this?" Orin asked as he pitched some snow into my face.

"No, I can't, but I sure am going to enjoy it." I wiped the snow from my face.

"Sean, I'll go first and you follow me," Orin said with a look of seriousness.

We had to make the path perfect, and Orin was an expert at creating great trails. Getting started was the hard part. Orin got on the tube and began rocking back and forth so that the tube began to move. Slowly he proceeded down the slope, leaving a deep trail behind him. I let him get at least halfway down, then began the same process. The trail was now well on its way to being completed.

When we both reached the bottom, we raced back to the top to enjoy the ride. Now that the snow on the path was packed, the tubes slid like rockets down the hill. You really had to be ready for a ride when you got on because once the tube started, there was no stopping it until you got to the bottom. Trip after trip the journey to the bottom became more and more swift. The air stung our faces as we zipped down the hill, but the rush was amazing.

Orin and I stayed on the hill until about noon when Dad came and told us to come in for lunch. As much as I hated to stop, I did because I was hungry and needed some dry clothes. My wardrobe had become soaked with melted snow after many crashes.

We put the inner tubes in the barn and made our way to the house. I was glad to see smoke bellowing out of the chimney, because I was frozen. When we arrived at the back porch, Orin and I took turns sweeping the snow off from one another with an old broom. Then we stepped into the laundry and stripped down to our long johns. Mom took our wet clothes and hung them all around the wood-burning stove to dry. We would use them again after they dried.

I quickly put on some dry clothes and made my way to the table to find that Mom had made chili. If there was ever a good day to eat chili, this was it. I needed all I could get to warm me up again. Orin finally found his way to the table, and after Dad prayed, we ate and talked about the glorious snow.

"I can't believe all of this snow so early in the season," I began.

"It is hard to believe, but I believe it." Mom chuckled.

"Are we supposed to get any more snow?" Orin asked with his mouth full of chili.

"The news said we could get four or five more inches by tomorrow morning, and we already have about ten inches," Dad answered.

I was overjoyed, because I knew beyond the shadow of a doubt that there would be no school tomorrow or maybe even the rest of the week. But I didn't want to get my hopes up.

"Dad, can we have a big bonfire tonight and sleigh ride after dark?" I asked.

"I don't see why not if you kids will help me get some things together to burn," Dad replied.

Immediately after eating, Hallie, Gil, Orin, and I went out to gather wood and junk to burn. We had done this a few years ago, and it was so fun that we were all willing to face the unseasonably cold weather in order to repeat the enjoyment.

After a sufficient amount of bonfire material was gathered, we spent the rest of the afternoon making snowmen, snow angels, and, of course, throwing snowballs. We were just waiting for the sun to go down so we could light the fire.

Despite all we had done, we somehow still had the energy to keep playing and playing. As the night began to fall, Mom brought Starr and Tempest out for a short time. They mostly sat near the soon-to-be bonfire, waiting for Dad to light it. We were already zooming down the hill and the twins loved to watch us. Dad, who had been watching like the leader of a pit crew ready to fix any and all holes created by a collision with a crab apple thorn or frozen cow pile, once again came to the rescue.

We had all learned that, on the first day, God had created light, but on this snowy night, Dad created "The Bonfire." After he lit the fire, the whole valley lit up. The light of the fire reflecting off the freshly fallen snow was amazing. Occasionally, we would stop long enough to roast a wiener or marshmallow. But we didn't waste a moment. The cold night air was filled with the *whoosh* of the tubes, the crackling of the fire, and the laughter of our family. It was a blessed time.

But just like all good times, this one went by too swiftly. Before we knew it, the fire was burning low, and we made our last trip down the hill. I hated to see the day end.

We trudged through the deepening snow to the house. As we went into the laundry to take off the wet clothes, Starr and Tempest broke out into hysterical laughter. They were pointing at Mom and when I looked at her I could see why they were laughing. Her face was covered in black soot from the fire. Upon closer examination I found that we had all become a bit charred-looking. We had a good laugh, then lined up for the bathroom, where we waited our turn for a warm shower.

As I lay in bed that night, I pondered the day gone by and decided that my family was a lot like those snowflakes falling outside. Just like all snowflakes are different from one another, so were families, and I had the most unique one God had ever created. I thanked God for my flaky family, then drifted off to the glorious thought that there would be no school tomorrow. Even better, my three-layer special would be dry by morning so I could spend yet another day in the snow.

33

'Twas the Weeks Before Christmas

Due to the early snowstorm, there was no school for the remainder of the week. I was somewhat relieved, but I knew that the days we missed would be added to the end of the school year. I made the best of the days, though. By the end of the week, nearly every slope on our farm was covered with trails that we'd made with our tubes. But then, just like all great things, the reign of snow had to end. The weekend temperatures rose into the 50s, so the snow didn't stand a chance.

On Sunday, Brother Force brought a message on Isaiah 1:18: "Come now, let us reason together, saith the Lord. Though your sins be as scarlet, they shall be as white as snow…."

That afternoon I realized our early winter break was about to come to an end. We would be back in school for three more weeks and then we'd be out for Christmas Break. I jotted down a quick verse of rhyme to give to Miss Frances because I knew she'd be impressed to know that I took the time to rhyme even when it was not required. Before I went to bed, Mom laid out a new outfit she'd bought for me since the tobacco had sold. My hand-me-down jeans were a bit holey for winter. I fell asleep that night with the *whoosh* of the tubes still nigh to my thoughts.

Monday began as a normal school morning until we got on the bus. Loretti was wearing makeup, and nearly all of the kids on the bus had on at least one new article of clothing. It was obvious that many farmers had sold their crops, and their children were getting early Christmas gifts. At school, the signs were obvious as well that many crops had been sold. I even saw a kid with a new lunchbox. Getting a new lunchbox midyear was unheard of.

When we were dismissed to our class, I dug in my pocket to find a little poem that I had jotted down for Miss Frances. It really wasn't much, but it had been quite some time since I had secured my reign as teacher's pet. She met us at the door, and I handed her the poem as I passed her in the threshold. She stood reading it and a smile began to blossom across her face. She cleared her throat and said, "Class, I'd like for you all to get to your seat as quickly as possible. I have something I would like to read to you."

The commotion in the room slowly softened, and Miss Frances began to read my poem.

"The following is a story of how the recent snow storm came to be.

One Snowflake said to another, 'We are alike, but yet not the same.'

The second inquired of the first, 'Did you know that we used to be rain?'

A third flake shouted, 'Wait up, I am coming too!'

Then a fourth flake shouted to the billions, 'Let's stick together and see what we can do.'"

Everyone in the class turned and looked at me. I just smiled. For the remainder of the day Miss Frances taught us lessons on money management, because she knew many of her students would be getting paid for work that they may have done during the course of the tobacco growing season. Many of the farmers in the area would ask that you wait until the crop sold to get your pay. I had never heard of anyone not getting paid.

Miss Frances even taught us how to write checks. My favorite part was signing my name. I signed it very large and distinct—sort of like how John Hancock signed *The Declaration of Independence.* I even wrote a check for $1,000,000. It sure felt good to write all of those numbers on the check. At lunch time, I jokingly gave the lunch lady a fake check for a week's worth of lunch. She just laughed.

After lunch we returned to the room to find Miss Frances speaking with a young boy not familiar to us. After we were seated, she said, "Class, I would like for you to meet our new student, Ian Best."

We all followed with, "Hello, Ian."

Miss Frances continued, "Ian comes to us from Harlan County. Let's all make him feel welcome."

The whole time he was being introduced, Ian never smiled or revealed any expression at all. He just studied us one at a time as if he were searching for someone. Miss Frances had him sit in the seat in front of me.

Ian had fine blonde hair and bright blue eyes. As he sat down, I noticed that he had no school supplies with him. His flannel shirt had seen better days and his boots were equally worn. He was wearing army fatigue pants with pockets on the legs. I always wanted a pair of those.

We reviewed how to write checks and balance the checkbook until recess. It had been raining all day, so we had inside recess. Miss Frances always had games or activities for us to do. Today we were to set up the Christmas tree. I helped drag the dusty old box out of the closet and then a small mob rushed to the box and began assembling our tree. The one kid in our class who could not read well, Philli Terate, had the instructions so I knew the end result would be a real beauty.

I noticed that Ian had not even got out of his seat, so I went over to speak with him. I held out my hand. "Hi, Ian. My name is Sean Merry."

He shook my hand. "Hey."

"So you're from Harlan County, heh?" I inquired.

"From coal country, you might say."

"Well, now you're in tobacco country," I joked.

Ian finally gave a half grin. "Yeah, that's what Mom told me as we were moving here. She said she wanted to get away from all of the heartache of the coalfields and come and live with my great-grandparents."

He went on to tell me that his dad had died in a coal mining accident the year before, and life had really become hard for him and his mom. She was doing all she could, but was so heartbroken that every coal truck that rattled through their little town made her cry. I could tell Ian's mother's sadness had also become his. I really felt bad for him. I made up my mind that I was going to do all I could to make Ian feel better.

During the course of our conversation, the Christmas tree was assembled, disassembled, and then reassembled twice because each time branches were obviously out of place. Finally, just as recess ended, the tree was complete. It was bare but complete.

The remainder of the day went by in a flash. At the very end of the day Miss Frances had each of us draw a name from a box for the Christmas gift exchange. I hoped and prayed I wouldn't draw a girl's name. One year I had to buy a gift for Cheney Booth, the most prissy girl in the class. I was so embarrassed when I went shopping for her gift. I spent most of the time hiding behind racks in the girls' department of the store while Mom shopped for the gift. Luckily I drew Jim "Mealworm" Meals' name. We called him Mealworm because he was so tall and skinny that he reminded us of a mealworm.

When the box made it to Ian and he pulled out the scrap of paper, he didn't even read it. He just put it in his pocket.

Before I knew it, and before I had a chance to say good-bye to Ian, the bell had rung and I was on the bus. All of the way home I couldn't help but think of Ian and how sad he was. I had to figure out a way to brighten his spirits.

That evening I talked to Dad about Ian. "We got a new kid in class today named Ian Best," I explained. "He's from Harlan County."

"Straight from coal country. What brings him here?" Dad inquired.

"He said he and his mom have come to live with his great-grandparents because his dad had been killed in a mine last year," I answered.

"That's so sad. You make sure you do all you can to be a good friend to him," Dad said.

"I was hoping you could help me think of a way to help brighten his spirits. He is the saddest person I've ever seen."

"I'll tell you what—you find out what the boy needs, and we'll see he gets it."

"I'll do my best," I answered.

I pondered my course of action until it was time for bed. Just before I fell asleep, I sat up in bed. "I've got it. I know just what I'll do."

"Now that you know what you are going to do, go to sleep!" Orin grumbled, not happy that I'd awakened him.

I said a prayer for Ian and his mom and fell asleep with my plan incubating in my mind.

34

The "Best" Plan

A long night of sleep helped me conjure up a great plan to help Ian. For the next two weeks I referred to it as the "Best" Plan. Any time I spoke about the plan I used the code name. It made me feel somewhat like a secret agent.

I spread the information about the "Best" Plan to each student in my class. I was sure to share it with Miss Frances as well, because she could help me prepare. Everyone was sworn to secrecy that they would not spoil my efforts.

The following Monday, only a week after I met Ian, I spent the entire recess talking with him about what he liked and disliked.

"So do you like it here?" I asked Ian.

"Yeah. Everybody seems to be real nice, and I love Smothers' store," Ian answered with a smile. His smiles were more common than they had been.

"You've been to Smothers'?" I asked.

"I walk there almost every day just to sit on the porch. It reminds me of a store back in Harlan County that my dad used to take me to. The door even squeaks the same way. There's also a lunch box on the wall like the one my dad used to take to the mines with him," he answered with a dreamy look as if he was picturing the other store.

"Do you live close to the store?" I continued.

"Just on the other side of the road on the old Moo More Dairy."

The old Moo More Dairy had been closed my whole life, but all of the tenant homes were still there. Later I found out that Ian lived in the largest of them. Apparently, his great-grandfather had been one of the original employees of the Moo More Dairy, and when the farm went out of business, he bought the largest tenant house.

The whole time that we talked I paid close attention to Ian's clothes. I was trying to size him up to see if he was about my size. It was all a part of the "Best" Plan. He appeared to be just a bit shorter and skinnier than me, but his feet were a different story. His shoes were at least 10s or 11s. I had never seen such feet on a kid. He'd sure stand up good in a windstorm.

I shared what I'd found out about Ian with my mom and dad. Mom was going to go make a visit to Ian's place and introduce herself to his mom. She also helped me dig through my closet and find some descent hand-me-downs to give to Ian. Even my most worn hand-me-downs were in better shape than any change of clothes that Ian had worn to school. I felt even more determined to help him.

The days passed by, and the "Best" Plan grew and grew. More and more people inquired about what they could do to help. Even the lunch ladies wanted to help.

Finally, the day had come to unveil the "Best" Plan for all to see. Most kids looked forward to Christmas break to get gifts and to get out of school. I was never so excited to go to school in my life.

The previous day Miss Frances had reminded everyone, "Students, don't forget to bring your gift for the passing party tomorrow."

I noticed that Ian had whispered something to Miss Frances shortly thereafter. She called my mom later on that evening and told my mom that Ian was concerned because he was unable to buy a gift. Miss Frances had assured him that things would be taken care of.

The next day the gym was full of students with gifts for their classmates and teachers. It looked as if Ian was the only student not bearing a gift. When we were dismissed to our class, everyone put their gift under the tree that was decorated with all kinds of ornaments that we had made in class.

For the entire morning we read a play version of *A Christmas Carol* by Charles Dickens. I was allowed to read the part of Ebenezer Scrooge. I did my best.

For lunch we had turkey, dressing, cranberry sauce, and cake. There were no lunch boxes in the whole cafeteria. Every child loved Christmas dinner at Roy G. Biv Elementary. Before we were dismissed back to class, Mrs. Whittle came into the gym and led the entire school while we sang every Christmas song from "Jingle Bells" to "Silent Night." There was joy in the air.

Miss Frances picked up our class shortly thereafter, and we went back to the classroom to prepare for our party. Miss Frances never had a problem with parties, but we had to do what she wanted in order to be able to have one. On that particular day we had to do an extensive cleaning of everything in the room. After the classroom was clean enough to pass her inspection, Miss Frances said, "I'd like everyone to push their seat to the back of the room. Then have a seat in the floor in front of the Christmas tree so we can open gifts." Immediately, we sprang into action and in a twinkle everyone was seated and ready.

"Ian, would you help me pass out the gifts, please?" Miss Frances asked.

Ian got up and, when he was in front of the tree with Miss Frances, she put a Santa Claus hat on him. He just grinned. "Just grab a gift," she said, "and read who the gift is for and give it to the student."

Ian nodded and went to work. He grabbed the first package. "Well now, if that isn't luck. I grabbed the gift someone bought for me. I'll save it for later," he said in surprise.

He reached for another and silently read the tag. He never said a word but instead looked at Miss Frances. She had tears in her eyes.

"To Ian Best," he read. He laid the package aside and grabbed another. "To Ian Best," he said again. Now Ian had tears in his eyes, because he realized that every student in the room had bought him a gift.

I was the first of many students who got up and totally surrounded Ian with the gifts that were around the tree. He was grinning from ear to ear. The "Best" Plan had been a success.

"Who thought of this?" Ian asked while he wiped his eyes.

Everybody pointed to me.

"You're my best friend. What'd you expect?" I told him.

Ian was the center of attention for the rest of the day. He opened gifts for over an hour. He got enough clothes so he'd not have to worry about wearing another hand-me-down the rest of the year. The last gift he opened was from me.

He picked it up and read the tag: "To Ian Best from Sean Merry."

He opened the package slowly and when he was able to see the gift, his eyes again filled with tears. The remaining paper fell from the gift to reveal the lunch box that he told me about that was hanging on the wall at Smothers' Grocery. He held it up for the whole class to see.

"It's just like my dad's," he sobbed.

There wasn't a dry eye in the room.

Little did Ian know, but across town, on what used to be called the Moo More Dairy, every mother who had a child in our classroom was throwing a welcoming party to a new resident who had just moved to our area from Harlan County. I could only imagine the joy that must have been circulating around that old dairy.

For the remainder of the day we sang more Christmas carols and ate some cookies that Miss Frances had made. Before the bell rang, we helped Ian pack all of his gifts to his bus. It took five whole seats to hold all of his treasures. As I lay down the last of the gifts, Ian put out his hand. "Thanks, Sean, for all you did. What a great surprise."

"That's what friends are for," I said and grinned.

We shook hands, and I got off the bus. I then made my way to the gym to await Loretti and bus 41. I was relieved everything had gone so smoothly. Most of all, I was glad everything did seem to really brighten Ian's countenance.

I found out later that day that Ian's mom had been equally surprised and thankful for the love of her new neighbors. I was certain it really had been the "Best" Plan.

35

A Honey of a Tree

Finally, our long-awaited Christmas break had arrived. The thrill of being able to surprise Ian and his mom was incredible. There had never been a happier or more surprised kid than Ian Best. I could still see his face when he realized that every present under the classroom tree was his. We were fortunate to live in such a small community where everyone loved everyone.

That night I prayed that Ian would be able to have a great Christmas break. Our family always had an annual celebration and dinner, but this year, I couldn't help but wonder if Ian would have anything other than what we had done at school.

The very next morning Mom began making preparations for Christmas, and so did I. You see, our family never was big on getting our Christmas tree up early like some people. I know that a lot of folks put up their tree the day after Thanksgiving, but we never put our tree up until school was let out for Christmas break.

That rule came about after Orin had a brilliant idea one year to put up the tree earlier than anyone around. He had cut down an overgrown pine sapling, put it in a bucket, and brought it inside. "It's hollow, but it'll do for a Christmas tree," he'd told us as he admired his find.

We decorated it and made that pathetic tree look decent. All was well for about three days...until something strange began to happen. Now you've got to remember that it was November, and it was cold outside.

Mom was busy cooking. Then, all of a sudden she started screaming, "OH, I'VE BEEN STUNG!" while doing a strange dance. Dad, as well as the rest of us, was bewildered. He sprang from his chair and ran into the kitchen, but before he made it, he let out a yell. "YOWEE! SOMETHING HAS STUNG ME TOO!"

I almost thought he was joking, but then I noticed Dad was swatting and dancing somewhat like Mom. Something weird was going on in the Merry household.

In the midst of his dance, Dad stopped and put his hand to his ear. "Do you all hear that?"

We each put our hands to our ears and listened intently. Sure enough, I could hear it. It was the buzzing of bees.

Dad's eyes got big, and he began sneaking through the house, following the buzzing sound. His search ended in the living room, where Orin had put the Christmas tree.

There, in our living room, was a full swarm of honeybees. They were everywhere. Some were buzzing in the windows, but most of them were swarming the tree.

Dad slowly turned and told us all to walk quietly to the closet and get our shoes and a coat because we had to get out of the house. We tiptoed quickly away and did as Dad had said. The whole time I could tell Orin was getting a little nervous, because he knew he was to blame.

Dad was the last one out of the house. "I called Carve, and he's gonna bring over his smoker and bee suits. We're gonna have to rob a bee tree in our own house," Dad finished with a chuckle. "Can you believe it? I just can't believe this! We've gotta rob our own house."

Uncle Carve showed up a few minutes later with all of his bee-keeping gear. It really was a funny sight. After Dad put on Carve's extra suit, they lit a smoker and went in. They used the smoker to drive the bees out of the house. I propped the door open, and we watched them through the window. Uncle Carve held the smoker, and Dad grabbed the tree. There must have been a million bees swarming in the living room, but Dad and Uncle Carve went unharmed because of the suits.

Then Dad came rushing out the door with the tree that was still swarming with bees, and Uncle Carve stayed behind to smoke the remainder of the bees toward the door. Dad whisked that tree far from the house and set it down. Talk about a strange sight. We had a fully decorated Christmas tree in our garden, and it was swarmed by bees.

Inside the house, Uncle Carve was slowly but surely moving the bees out. After about thirty minutes, he came out and declared, "We have exorcised the bees!"

We burst out into chilly laughter.

Mom and the girls went back into the smoky house and opened the windows to let out the leftover smoke. Dad and Uncle Carve went to work removing the honey from the tree. The now frozen bees were mostly gone or moving really slow.

"We'll see what's inside this tree," Dad said as he began chopping on the tree. He cut a large notch in the tree's trunk until he struck gold. "Honey! We've got honey!" Dad shouted.

That day we filled three pint jars with honey from a Christmas tree. It was memorable.

But now you see how the "No tree until Christmas break" rule came to be in the Merry household.

Many months prior to Christmas I had spotted a pine sapling up in the cow pasture that was to be our tree. It wasn't as perfect as the ones they sold down at the lot next to Gracie Brothers, but it would do.

I got up long before Orin but had to wait on him to get up because I couldn't drag the tree off the hill by myself. To pass the time I went to the barn, found the few boxes marked *Christmas Stuff,* and brought them to the house.

I put the boxes in the living room where the tree would be and opened one to begin sorting the ornaments. Dad had always said that Mom never could throw anything away, and this box was evidence of that statement. There were trinkets and paper ornaments all the way back to when Gil was in kindergarten. Mom always said they had sentimental value, so every one of them was placed somewhere on the tree each year.

The next box I opened was full of lights. I closed the lid quickly because checking the lights to see if they worked was enough to drive a boy insane. I'd leave that job for Dad or Orin.

I could finally hear Orin yawning and stretching like an old bear coming out of hibernation. Boy, he looked rough when he finally showed up.

"Are you gonna wake up and help me get our tree off the hill or what?" I asked him.

"I'll help you in MY time!" he snapped back.

"Well, I hope your time is before Christmas," I answered.

Orin just hit me in the arm and made his way to the kitchen to get a bite to eat. I made one last trip to the barn to bring in another box, and by the time I got back to the house Orin was putting on his boots. After getting his boots on, Orin stood and made one more stretch before heading to the door.

As we stepped out, a few snow flurries drifted in the air.

"Where's the tree you picked out?" Orin asked.

"In the back pasture near the pond."

"I guess that's not too far," Orin grumbled.

I grabbed the hatchet, and we trudged up the hill. Along the way we saw all sorts of creatures.

"Boy, I wish I would have brought the shotgun," Orin said as a couple of gray squirrels ran up a nearby tree.

Soon we arrived at the pond, and I pointed the tree out to Orin.

"That's a sorry looking tree if I've ever seen one," Orin said with a smirk.

"At least I checked and there's no danger of us being stung to death by a family of bees living inside it!" I barked back.

The bee incident was still a sore spot with Orin, so he didn't reply.

I let Orin cut the tree down. It didn't take long before the little tree began to lean and we both yelled, "TIMBER!" as it fell. We each got on one side of the tree and began to drag it off the hill. Those were the purest of times.

When we arrived home, the girls were up and ready to help decorate the tree. Mom met us at the door and inspected the tree for any unwanted critters. Gil filled a small pail with water. Slowly we made our way to the living room, placed the tree's trunk in the pail, and stood it up. Starr and Tempest applauded as the tree stood upright for the first time. My hands were covered in sticky sap.

Dad, who had been gone to the cattle market all morning, pulled into the driveway just as we stood the tree up. He peeked into the living room. "I don't need a bee suit to come in here, do I?"

Orin said nothing, but the rest of us laughed.

"Dad, we need you to put the lights on the tree so we can decorate it," Hallie called out.

You see, we knew we had to get Dad involved immediately, or he'd go off somewhere and do something else.

Dad did the honors of untangling the lights, then neatly draped them around and around the tree. Each of us sorted through the many boxes of decorations to find ones we'd made, and then we placed them on the tree. Every ornament that went onto the tree added a little more of a personal touch. There were only a few that had been bought, but the rest were home- or school-made. Starr and Tempest had the fewest ornaments, so we allowed them to hang some of ours.

I never told anyone, but at that moment I started to feel a sensation that was hard to explain. I felt so thankful that my whole family was right there in the same house for the same purpose. Poor Ian. Oh, how I hoped he could somehow feel the same way.

After about two hours of decorating, the last ornament had to be placed at the highest point. Mom and Dad had bought a star for their first Christmas tree, and we still used it. Mom stored it in a wrapped box that she kept in her closet. Now she opened the box gingerly and parted the tissue in the box to reveal the star. Even after all these years, it still looked brand-new.

"Starr and Tempest," Dad said, "you girls get the honors."

They both ran to Dad, and he placed one on each of his shoulders. After Dad stood up, Mom handed the star to the twins and Dad walked over to the tree. The twins held onto the star. They reached toward the tip of the tree and slipped it over the branch. Instant celebration followed. Our tree was now complete.

Dad went on to tell us, as he did annually, about that bright star that showed the way for the shepherds to find our Lord Jesus there in Bethlehem.

Tempest spoke after Dad had finished. "Sing baby Jesus song!"

We sang "Away in a Manger" about thirty times, then Starr insisted that Dad say a prayer. So Dad led us in a short prayer.

"Dear God, May we honor You in this season and in every season. We pray that You will protect us and give us many more blessed times here in this place. I ask this in Jesus' name, Amen."

I could not have said it better myself.

36

The Greatest Gift

There are some things that are hard to put into words and the joy of each Christmas in our house was one of them. It was the one time of year that Dad spent more time around the house rather than working. Yeah it was cold out and the weather wasn't fit for working, but Dad just wanted to make the best of the season.

We never did get wrapped up in the decorating and big gift buying hoopla that so many others did. In fact, the only decorating we did was putting up the tree. Now that it was complete, all we had to do was enjoy our time together. Despite what some would call a meager celebration, there was a feeling of pure joy growing in the air.

Every year both sets of grandparents—Dad's parents, the Merrys, and Mom's parents, the Groves—would come and have Christmas dinner with us. We would also make a visit to Mr. Malone. He didn't like to get out in the cold weather, so we'd take him a little treat. His gratitude was unbelievable. We loved him like he was part of our own family.

There had even been a few occasions where other people from church and an occasional relative would come and spend Christmas with us. But no matter how many people showed up, we always had enough love and joy to go around.

One other tradition we had was one that only our immediate family took part in—and always on Christmas Eve. A few days prior, Dad would begin to remind us, "Don't forget to count your blessings." You see, every year right before bedtime on Christmas Eve, Dad would read the story of Jesus' birth from Luke chapter two. Then, after he finished, he would always say, "You see, the greatest gifts come from God." He would then ask each one of us to share one gift that God had given us throughout the year. I already knew what I was going to say, and I couldn't wait. But I had to. There were still three days until Christmas.

In the meantime, we'd play family games and then we'd go to church on Sunday. Just like all other school vacations, Christmas break went by in a wink, a blink, and a nod.

Sunday came around quickly. The morning air was crisp, I knew, because I had to go out and get some wood for the fire when I got up. I put a few pieces of wood on the fire and stood closely to the stove to try to kill the chill. The old stove warmed me up in a jiffy.

Dad must have heard me putting the wood into the stove because he came down the hall and peered around the corner. "Good morning, Sean."

I answered with the same greeting. Dad made his way over to the coffee pot to brew some high-octane coffee.

After getting the coffee brewing, Dad turned to me. "Have you been counting your blessings?"

"I have, and I lost count," I jokingly replied.

"Well, you better remember at least one great one to share on Christmas Eve," Dad insisted.

"Oh, don't you worry. I'll be ready," I assured Dad.

By then, Mom and the twins were awake. Mom's specialty would be star-shaped pancakes—to represent the Star of David, of course. Starr and Tempest went straight to the living room to rearrange the ornaments on the tree. It was a ritual that they had every morning and I had no intentions of interfering.

By the time Mom was able to make a half dozen stars, the rest of the crew woke up. Once again, sleep sure had not been kind to Orin. Everyone settled around the table, and Mom began putting the specialty pancakes on our plates. After each of us had two pancakes, Mom sat down and Dad asked the blessing on the food.

Now that I was getting a little bigger, Mom recognized my need for extra helpings and, let me tell you, they were greatly appreciated.

At about 9:30, Dad started the car to let it warm up. We left as soon as the frost thawed from the windshield. I watched out the window as we passed the tobacco fields, barns, and pastures. When we passed Mr. Malone's house, there was a steady stream of smoke coming from his chimney, which was a good sign that he was up. He was unable to go to church that morning because the cold air was really hard on him.

We pulled into the church lot at the same time as Billy and Blenda. Billy was driving Blenda's car, and somehow he didn't look right sitting behind the wheel of a car. He was more of a truck kinda guy. Dad and Billy greeted each other with a handshake while Mom and Blenda embraced each other with a neighborly hug. I headed straight to the door, because the air was extra cold.

Brother Force opened the door for me. As I entered and gave him the customary handshake, he put a candy cane in my shirt pocket. "Good morning, Sean Merry. How are you?"

"I'm doing great," I replied as I excitedly pulled the candy cane from my pocket. Starr and Tempest squealed as he gave them their candy cane. I made my way to Brother Leroy in order to make my annual song request. As I walked toward the front I noticed that everyone was sitting near the middle of the church. We had saved up enough money to put in a gas floor furnace, and everyone wanted to feel its warmth.

Brother Leroy saw me approaching. "I'll bet you want to sing a bunch of Christmas songs, don't you?"

"You know me awfully well, Brother Leroy." I smiled.

"Tell you what. We'll sing nothing but Christmas songs today."

"Thank you, Brother Leroy." I shook his warm hand.

I made my way back to the pew where the twins were crunching on their candy canes like a couple of starved orphans. Orin was still trying to open his. Just then Brother Leroy and Sister Force made their way to the front and we stood to sing, "Away in a Manger" and five other traditional Christmas songs before Brother Force went to the pulpit to preach.

He began with a question. "How would you feel if I gave you a gift box, and when you opened it, there was nothing in it?"

Only silence followed. Orin leaned to me. "Wouldn't that be a terrible gift?"

I nodded in agreement.

Brother Force broke the silence. "Well, to tell you the truth, the greatest gift I ever received was an empty package."

Now he had the attention of everyone in the building. Even Starr and Tempest were looking up from their half-eaten candy canes.

"I'm certain there are thousands of preachers preaching on the Birth of Christ at this very moment. Now don't get me wrong, but His birth was not His greatest gift. You see, the greatest gift was when His followers went to His grave and found nothing."

Brother Force preached basically the same sermon that he preached on Easter Sunday but with a different angle. He illustrated to us clearly how that we should be thankful that Jesus' followers did not find Jesus in that tomb because it proved that He had power over the grave. I had never before thought that an empty gift could be of any value until that day.

At the end of the service, we sang "Shall We Gather At the River," and the whole time I couldn't help but think that if we gathered at the river today, we could all ice skate because it would be frozen over. Judging by the smile on Orin's face, he was thinking the same thing. After the song had ended, Brother Force made the announcement that there would be no evening service because there was an impending snow storm on its way. Since he lived so far away, he felt it was best to be safe rather than sorry. After Brother Leroy dismissed us with prayer, we exited the church.

A few lazy snow flurries were floating toward the ground and the air still had a bite to it. I ran to the car so I could get out of the frigid wind. Nobody stood outside and talked long. It was much too cold.

On the way home Dad stopped by Mr. Malone's to see if all was well. While there, Dad put a little more wood on the fire, and Orin and I carried some more wood inside so Mr. Malone wouldn't have to. We always took care of him any way that we could. Dad told Mr. Malone we'd bring him some lunch in about an hour. His face lit up, because he always did like Mom's cooking. Then we said our good-byes and made our way home.

We were glad to see that there was still smoke coming from our chimney, because that meant the house would be nice and warm. Smif came running around the house. He was extra spunky, I guess, to help him keep warm. He ran alongside me while I ran to the door and waited for Dad to come unlock it. As soon as the key was turned, we pressed in and stood near the stove.

The house smelled like chili because Mom had cooked it before we went to church. She'd also stacked bowls and a handful of spoons on the counter. It looked like a buffet at a fancy restaurant. You grabbed a bowl and a spoon and then filled the bowl yourself. Dad had an extra large bowl. Everyone but Starr and Tempest filled their own bowl. Gil and Mom filled theirs. We all managed to get seated, then Dad offered the blessing on the food. In addition to asking God to bless the food, Dad also thanked God for leaving us with an empty tomb to show that Jesus had arisen.

When Dad said, "AMEN," I crumbled up a handful of crackers and enjoyed my chili. It was only two days until Christmas, and I had not heard Mom or Dad talk about any company that we might have.

"Mom," I asked, "Is anyone coming for Christmas dinner this year?"

"Well, I know that Papaw and Mamaw Grove and Papaw and Mamaw Merry are planning to be here, but I don't know about anyone else," she answered while she held a spoonful of chili in the air to cool off.

"So will they be staying overnight?" Hallie asked.

"I guess we'll know when they get here," Mom replied.

When we had overnight company, Orin and I would sleep on the living room floor, and Gil and Hallie would sleep on the couches. We made do.

Dad made his last reminder, "Now don't you all forget to be ready to share one blessing that God has given you this past year. Tomorrow will be here before you know it. In fact, since we don't have church tonight, you probably should write it down so that you don't forget it."

Few words were spoken after that point, I guess, because we were all thinking about which blessing we would share. After finishing our chili, we left the table. Dad put some chili in a quart jar and took it to Mr. Malone as he had promised.

In the meantime, I went to my room. Despite the fact that I knew I would not forget which blessing I wanted to share, I still wrote it down.

Only one more day and we'd get to share our blessings. Just one more day. I couldn't wait, but I had to.

37

Count Your Blessings

I suppose that, in the heart of a child, Christmas could never come too soon. In all reality, it seemed that last year's Christmas had barely passed, and now the season was upon us again. That Sunday night I could not sleep, much like the night before school began, and I knew I would be even more restless tomorrow night, Christmas night.

I woke up early that Christmas Eve morning. Mom had already filled the house with the aroma of pumpkin pie, and there was a huge bowl of bread dough rising on the countertop. The bread grew like it was going to explode. I know Miss Frances had said that it had something to do with yeast and that it was alive. That was a bit weird, if you ask me. I made my way over to the fridge, where I found my favorite holiday treat, eggnog. I don't know why the stores only sold eggnog around Christmas time, but the wait made it taste all the better. Only Dad and I would drink it. It made Hallie and Gil gag to watch me guzzle the thick drink. I had one glass and filled another to wash down my breakfast.

"Mom, when are Papaw and Mamaw Grove gonna be here?" I asked as I pulled up a chair and put my cup of Christmas cheer on the table.

"They said that they'd be here around eight or nine tomorrow morning."

"What about Mamaw and Papaw Merry?"

"All that I know is that they're supposed to be here for lunch." Mom pulled a fresh pie out of the oven.

Mom put the pie on a bureau next to two others. They were baked to a beautiful amber color. Mom also made two little pumpkin pies for

Starr and Tempest. She always saved two tins from pot pies in which to make the baby pies.

About that time, Dad walked in the back door with an armload of wood. He put it in the wood box that was by the door. "It's certainly winter out there today!" Dad shivered.

"But it's warm in here, thanks to you," Mom said.

Dad put a piece of wood on the fire and stood nearby its warmth until the ruddiness left his cheeks. If I was not mistaken, I could smell the slightest hint of exhaust on him. It had a real oily/smoky smell to it. I never inquired about the smell but instead went to the living room, where the Christmas tree was. I checked the bucket and made sure the tree had plenty of water. Despite its humble beginnings, the tree was quite pretty. There were a few presents under it. Mom and Dad always bought one or two gifts for each of us and one for each other. For the rest of us, we usually bought or made a little something for each other. We were very practical. I can remember one year where Papaw and Mamaw Grove gave each of us an apple and an orange. It was more than we deserved, and we were grateful.

I had gone to Smothers with Dad the week earlier and bought a few sticks of candy for Orin and the girls. I got Dad a new handkerchief and Mom a little sewing kit that had a few needles, buttons, and thread for small sewing emergencies. At the rate I was growing, I was always popping off buttons and splitting stitches so the gift would be good for me as well.

For most of the day I sat and read the book *Treasure Island.* I read the part about when young Jim Hawkins met the poor marooned sailor, Ben Gunn. Poor old Ben had been left on the island to die, and Jim was the first person he'd seen in a long time. I thought it must be a terrible feeling to be all alone. I thought again of Ian Best and his mother. Oh, how I hoped they weren't alone. Again, a feeling of gratefulness for my family swept over me.

Before the evening passed into darkness, Orin and I went outside to feed the animals and pack in firewood. There was a dusting of snow on the sidewalk—just enough to make walking with an armload of wood tricky. We managed to get all of our chores done without falling.

Once back inside, I could hear the rattle of plates and utensils. We sat down that evening to an evening breakfast. I loved whenever Mom would cook the traditional breakfast foods for lunch or dinner. They tasted great anytime.

After Dad said the prayer, the dinner conversation was almost nonexistent. I think everyone was thinking about what blessing they were going to share with the family after dinner. I was still rock solid for sure what I was going to share. After about fifteen minutes, everyone had eaten their fill.

Dad broke the silence. "All right, everyone to the living room," he said while pushing in his chair. "It's time to share what the Lord has done for us this past year."

We all followed suit and followed Dad into the living room where the tree was lit up so pretty. After everyone assumed a position near the tree, Dad again read Luke chapter 2 and told us, "God sent His Son to us and His birth was the most wonderful birth ever. We've read about what God did for us, now let's share how God has continued to bless us."

It was customary for Dad to begin. "God has blessed me with a great family. The greatest blessing that God has given me this past year is yet another attribute of my great family. I love the way we can work together and, despite the hard times, we push and pull until we are through it. And, best of all, we all come through it together."

There was only a brief silence until Hallie spoke up. "God has blessed me this year by helping me do better in school. He has also helped me realize that there is a lot more to life than just living."

Mom was the next to share. "God has blessed me by allowing me to watch all of my kids grow up so beautifully. I am so grateful to have each of you, and you too, of course, Arden."

Orin spoke next. He stood up just to make it a little more dramatic. "God has given me a lot of blessings this year. First, he has helped me through the first half of my freshman year of high school without getting into trouble. Secondly, if you haven't noticed, I'm growing up and am nearly as tall as Dad."

We could all see where Orin's speech was going, so we pulled him back down to the floor so that he would hush.

Gillian spoke up quickly so Orin would realize his time was up. "God has blessed me by helping me accept more responsibilities and carry them out in a good way. I also feel that He is giving me direction for when I graduate this spring. In fact, I've decided to go to college next fall."

This was the first time that Gil had spoken about her post-graduation plans. Mom and Dad looked at her proudly. If she really did go to college, she would be the first of the Merry family to do so.

At that time, I seized the moment and shared my blessing. "I know that God gives us blessings each day, but there was one this year that I cannot get past. Sure, we had a great year with the crops and not to mention we found the biggest ginseng root ever, but those things don't even compare with my big blessing." I could tell everyone was compelled to listen.

"This year, when Ian Best came to school and I learned of his tragic circumstances, my heart hurt in a way that it never had before. I really felt sorry for him and his mom and knew that I had to do something to help them. God blessed me by helping me to realize that it really is better to give than to receive. I was never so happy to give in all my life. That was the best blessing of all."

Mom wiped tears from her eyes, and I think that Dad did too.

It was time for the twins to share, but they were both asleep. Tempest was in Dad's arms, and Starr was in Mom's.

"I know that God has a lot more blessings where those came from. We just have to be living for Him," Dad said.

After that short time together, we knew and loved each other a little more. I could have gone on forever about the blessings that God had given me. One thing I'd failed to mention was that I'd never learned that it was better to give than to receive on my own. My family had instilled that value in me. I was just able to experience it for the first time from the giving side.

Next we sang a chorus of the little song, "Count Your Blessings."

"Count your blessings name them one by one;
Count your blessings see what God hath done.
Count your blessings, name them one by one.

Count your many blessings see what God hath done."

After the song, we got ready for bed. Tomorrow would be a busy day.

I went to bed thinking about the night and the blessings that were shared. I prayed that night that Ian Best and his mother, wherever they were, would have the greatest Christmas ever. As Orin turned off the lights, I could see a few flakes of snow falling lazily past our window.

I lay only a short time with the little song chorus still ringing in my head. I decided to take the little song literally and began to count my blessings. I counted ten, then twenty, and then somewhere between twenty-one and thirty, I fell asleep. Counting blessings worked much better than counting sheep.

38

A Merry Christmas (Part I)

As we slept that night, lots of things were happening all around us and we didn't even know it. Magic, some may say. Gifts were appearing under trees, sugar plums were dancing in people's heads and to make things a little more Christmas-like, it was pouring down the snow. Of course I had no clue of this until Orin awakened me at about three in the morning. He was shaking my bed like a madman.

"Wake up, Sean!" he was whispering.

My eyes finally opened, and there was Orin right in my face with a flashlight in his hand. I knew why he was waking me, but his unconventional waking tactics were awful. I sat up in bed and let my feet fall to the floor with a kerplunk. Orin then guided me through the hallway and to the living room with his flashlight. When we entered the living room he flipped on the light switch. Initially, I was blinded but recovered quickly to see several gifts in front of the Christmas tree.

That strange sensation that tingled in my stomach was back. I ran to the tree and began reading the names. The names were so obscure and hard to find and the handwriting was awful. Finally, I turned over a large box and there was my name, written sloppily on a snowman's belly. I picked up the package and shook it a little. There was only a slight rattle. Orin was also shaking a package that had his name on it. We knew we couldn't open the gifts until everyone got up, but it was still fun to shake them and guess what was inside.

Orin looked at me. "Should we go ahead and wake everyone?"

"Orin, Dad would wring our necks if we woke him up right now."

We both went back to our beds to sleep a little longer. As I turned off the light, I noticed that it was snowing and it had actually accumulated about an inch. Mom always loved a white Christmas.

I lay down on my pillow, hoping I could fall asleep but I only wanted to sleep a little while. This was the one night of the year that I hoped Dad would get up super early, but the contrary was always true. Dad had a way of sleeping longer on Christmas morning. There were times that I thought he did it on purpose, but I guess if anyone deserved some extra sleep it was my dad.

It seemed that my eyes had only closed for a second before I was waking up again. This time I knew that Mom was up because I could smell bacon cooking and coffee perking. I doubted that Dad was up. Despite my doubts, I got up and wondered into the living room, bypassing the kitchen. There, on the floor, was Orin, fast asleep.

I looked outside, and the snow had stopped falling. There were about three inches on the ground. Not much but still, it was snow.

Orin raised his head and asked, "Is Dad up yet?"

"No but I hear the girls getting up so maybe we can use the twins to wake him," I replied.

As Starr and Tempest came running down the hall, I motioned for them to come into the living room. They squealed with excitement and ran to the tree to look at all the gifts. I had already set all of their gifts aside in one pile.

"Do you girls want to open your presents?" I tantalizingly asked.

They both replied with a unanimous, "YES!"

Now that I had them enthused, I had to seize the moment and send them to wake Dad. It was my only hope.

"You girls know that we can't open any gifts until Dad gets up, so you need to go wake him," I told them.

They both nodded. Then they looked at each other and ran down the hall. I could hear them jump on Dad's bed. What went on in there must have been really effective because I heard Dad's feet hit the floor almost immediately. I left the living room so Dad wouldn't suspect I'd sent the twins to wake him.

Dad walked down the hall with the twins leading him by his hands. They pulled him into the living room and the squealing recommenced. Gil and Hallie both entered the living room to see what all of the commotion was about. They were well past the age where they got excited about the gifts. Oh, how I hoped that I'd never be that way.

"Breakfast is ready," Mom informed us.

We went to the table to enjoy a biscuit, gravy, and bacon breakfast. After Dad said the prayer, we ate like starved children. We certainly were not starved, but we wanted to finish quickly so we could open gifts. Dad never rushed, but he did finish quicker than usual.

Dad must have known the excitement was almost enough to kill us. After he filled his cup with coffee, he made his way to the living room so we could open gifts.

The twins got to open a gift first. They each had a box that was wrapped identically. As soon as their hands touched the boxes, the girls began tearing off the paper. Tempest was more aggressive than Starr and had her gift opened first.

"A baby!" Tempest squealed. At the same time, Starr revealed her gift as well.

Now Orin and I would open a gift. I grabbed my middle-sized gift and Orin grabbed his smallest. I tore off the paper and inside there was a toy replica of a Massey Ferguson tractor with a cab. What a dream! A tractor with a cab. Orin found a nice shiny pocket knife in his package. Gil and Hallie opened a gift and each of them received new night gowns and a bath robe.

During the gift unwrapping bonanza, Mom and Dad just watched and smiled. Each of us had three gifts this year.

The twins opened one gift that was for both of them. It was a large package and inside they found a baby cradle for their dolls. We also let them open their last gift, which turned out to be strollers for their dolls.

I wanted to open my smallest gift, so I readied myself and tore into the package. Inside I found a small red wagon that could be pulled by my Ferguson replica. It looked a lot like wagons that I had seen down at Gracie Brothers. Orin opened his largest gift and it was a new bike. It was not put together, but he loved to assemble things. He began putting it together immediately. Gil and Hallie opened their last two gifts. In one package they found a new pair of jeans and a blouse in the other.

All that was left was one gift for me and one for Orin. Orin opened his gift first and inside he found a pair of coveralls. I opened a similar package and found some coveralls inside as well. Despite the fact that the house was toasty warm, we both had to put our coveralls on so that Mom could make sure they fit us right. They were a bit big, but we lived by the "You'll grow into it" philosophy. After Mom approved, we could take the coveralls off. I had broken a sweat in just the few minutes I had them on.

Mom and Dad exchanged gifts after we finished. Dad brought in a medium-sized box for Mom. There were a couple of small packages that went along with it as well. She opened the first and unveiled a new 35mm camera. The other boxes had film and lenses in them. Mom's eyes filled with tears. She immediately put some film in the camera and began a barrage of flashes. After taking a picture of each of us, Mom asked Dad, "Arden, do you want your gift now, or do you want me to wait until your parents get here?"

"Well, I guess since you have already opened your gift, then I should open mine," Dad replied.

"You all wait right here. I have to make a phone call," Mom said as she left the room.

I was too busy playing with my tractor and wagon to think anything of Mom making a call on Christmas Day.

While Mom was in the other room, Dad got in the floor and played with the twins. Orin continued to put his bike together. Mom finally came back into the room empty-handed and grinning from ear to ear.

"Where's my gift?" Dad joked. "Is it so small that I can't see it?"

"It's kinda hard arranging a special delivery on Christmas Day. It'll be here shortly," Mom coolly replied.

Now we were all on pins and needles, wondering what in the world Mom had done. Dad, who was hard to surprise, seemed a bit curious. In fact, he was very curious. Curious enough to begin asking Mom rapid-fire questions.

"Where is it? What is it? What have you done? Is this some kind of joke?"

Mom never buckled under the pressure. Instead she snapped a few pictures of Dad's curious face.

In the midst of the commotion, Tempest asked, "What's that noise?" We all stopped and listened. There was a rumbling sound coming from outside. As we listened, it grew louder.

"Your gift has arrived, Arden, but you can't see it just yet," Mom said while she rushed to the door. We could tell that she meant for us to stay behind as well so we just stayed seated. The roaring stopped in front of the house. We listened closely. The thud of two doors closing was the only sound in the air. Curiosity was at the maximum by this point.

Then Mom hurried back in and put a blindfold on Dad's eyes. We helped Dad slip on some shoes and a jacket, then Mom led him out the door. Not properly dressed for the winter weather, each of us tiptoed behind Mom. Mom had asked us to not look at the gift as well. So each of us walked with our eyes to the ground. We walked to the edge of the driveway, then Mom stopped and said, "On the count of three, you can look up."

"One, Two, THREE!" Mom counted while pulling the blindfold from Dad's eyes.

All of us looked up to see a shiny red Massey Ferguson on the Gracie Brothers' flatbed truck. Big and Little Gracie were both standing there all bundled up. I could tell they were both smiling.

No one, not even Orin, could speak.

"It's not new," Mom said, "but it'll sure help Ole Red get some much needed rest."

Dad advanced toward the tractor. "It's beautiful! I just couldn't decide if we should get one or not."

Mom smiled. "That's why I went ahead and got it because I knew you wouldn't."

"Where can we unload it?" Big Gracie asked.

Dad snapped back to reality. "Just back over against the hillside where we load cattle."

Little Gracie hopped up into the driver's seat and backed the truck up to the hillside. You could hardly see him above the wheel, and he stretched to see in the mirrors as he backed up. The old truck bumped up against the hillside and came to a stop.

Both the Gracies began unchaining the tractor, and Dad climbed into the driver's seat. He was like a kid with a new toy.

"Arden, even as cold as it is, you won't have to use any ether with this tractor. It has warmers in the cylinders that get her warmed up so she'll start quickly," Little Gracie said.

After the last chain was unhooked, Dad turned the key halfway until a light signifying the tractor was ready to start came on. With that, he turned the key and just like magic, the Ferguson blew out a puff of gray smoke and fired right up. We all cheered like Dad had won some sort of a race.

Dad studied the gears for a moment, found reverse, and backed the tractor off the truck. The cheering continued. I had never seen Dad so happy. I'm sure that if a stranger would have driven by and seen our whole family standing in the snow watching Dad drive a tractor, they would have thought we had escaped from the loony bin.

Dad turned off the tractor, and we went over to inspect what became known as "New Red." The paint was bright and hardly showed signs of weathering. It was obvious this tractor had been kept in the dry. "I can't believe that you actually bought this!" Dad said to Mom. Mom just smiled. She then took the twins inside so they wouldn't freeze to death. I was cold as well, but my excitement would keep me warm enough to survive.

"Dad, this is awesome!" Orin shivered.

"This is just what we've needed." I shivered.

"Did you know Mom was getting this for you?" Gil asked while shivering.

Dad shivered his reply. "I had no idea."

Big and Little Gracie were the only ones not shivering because they had on coveralls. I thought to myself how nice my new coveralls would feel right now, but I had forgotten them in all the excitement.

Little Gracie said, "Arden, Merry Christmas. I hope you get some use out of this rig. And by the way, get those kids in the house before they freeze over."

Dad replied with a "Thank you" and dismounted the tractor to shake the Gracie Brothers' hands. They then got into their truck and drove away. Dad hopped onto his new tractor and drove it toward the barn, where he would park it in the lower shed. The tires left nice deep tracks in the snow that formed peculiar patterns. I watched for only a minute, then led the exodus back to the house. Heat never felt so good. I had to stand by the stove for quite some time before all the chill was out of my bones.

Dad finally came in, and he looked a bit frozen as well. We made room for him next to the stove.

I'm sure we were all thinking the same thing, "This is the best Christmas ever, and the day has only begun."

And we were right.

39

A Merry Christmas (Part II)

How could a day like this get any better? I couldn't help but wonder. The old stove had successfully warmed me through and through, so I went to the living room to play with my new Massey Ferguson tractor replica and wagon. The toy was strikingly similar to the one that Dad had just been given. Orin was putting the finishing touches on his bike, and the twins were pushing their baby dolls around in their carriage. Gil and Hallie were helping Mom get the food ready for lunch.

It was almost ten o'clock when Mamaw and Papaw Grove drove slowly up the road. The snow had only accumulated a little on the road, so they were able to come to lunch. Papaw drove slowly anyway and since there was snow on the roads, he drove even slower.

"Orin, Mamaw and Papaw Grove are here. Let's go help them in," I told him. Besides, this would give us an opportunity to break in our new coveralls.

After getting dressed, we went to the car and there stood Papaw holding Mamaw's arm. It was a priceless picture.

"Hold on, Papaw," I began. "Let me help her, and Orin can help you get the rest of the stuff."

I made my way over to Mamaw and took her by the arm.

"Sean, you are growing like a weed in the springtime," Mamaw said.

"I hope I keep right on growing for a while," I replied.

I walked her carefully up the drive. Mamaw was nowhere near feeble, but I just didn't want to risk her falling. We entered the house and the twins ran to greet Mamaw Grove. She bent down to greet them, then made her way to the kitchen to help out with the cooking. The hen chatter began immediately.

Meanwhile, Orin was helping Papaw bring in a bag of gifts and a dish of food. As Papaw came in, he received a similar reception from the twins as Mamaw did. He swept the twins up into his arms and went to the living room and plopped down on the couch. He was a very strong looking man who had been discharged from the army after only eight weeks of service because he broke his leg in an accident on the military base. "I don't guess I would have made a difference in Uncle Sam's ranks," he'd said. "There were more than enough boys to take care of Hitler's Germany." He still walked with a slight limp, but he never let it get in the way of him working and doing what everyone else did.

Dad was nowhere to be found at this time. We all knew that he was up at the barn looking at his new tractor. I went up to the barn to look at his gift as well.

I walked in Dad's footprints that he had left in the snow. It wasn't as hard for me to make the large strides anymore.

When I walked into the barn, Dad was putting some clips and necessary tools in the new Ferguson's toolbox.

"So what do you think of it, Dad?" I asked him.

"It sure is a fine looking tractor, and it'll give Ole Red some much needed rest," Dad replied while patting the hood of the tractor.

"We're gonna keep Ole Red, aren't we?" I asked.

Dad replied with a nod. "I don't think I could part with Ole Red. Besides, we can keep him for light duties and hillside work."

I walked over to Ole Red and climbed up onto the seat. I didn't want him to feel betrayed. As soon as I sat down, I heard someone talking. I listened closely and realized that Papaw and Mamaw Merry had arrived. I had not heard the gravel popping under the tires because of the snow but I could certainly hear Papaw talking. He had a voice that could cut hardened steel. Ironically, he had retired from a steel mill just ten years earlier.

He wasn't even in the barn yet and he yelled, "Arden! Aren't you a bit old for getting toys at Christmas time?" He finished with his trademark bellowing laugh.

"This here tractor is no toy. It's a tool," Dad called back and turned to greet Papaw.

I hopped off the tractor and went over to hug Papaw. He put his arm around me and placed his hand on my shoulder. His hands were mammoth compared to mine. All of those years at the steel mill had made him a brute. Just like Papaw Grove and almost every aged man in the community, Papaw Merry had also served in the military during World War II. Papaw Merry did go to Europe and fought in a few battles in France and Belgium near the end of the war.

"Sean, from the looks of things your dad is really gonna have to raise a lot of burley to pay for his new toy," Papaw joked.

"It's a tool," Dad muttered.

"Let's argue about it later. Lunch is ready, and I'm hungry," Papaw said while turning away.

Dad and I followed him to the house. As soon as the door opened, I could smell the wonderful scent of Christmas dinner and all its garnishes. Both Mamaw Grove and Mamaw Merry were sitting on the couch talking about who knows what and Papaw Grove was still playing with the twins.

"I found Sean and Arden up at the barn petting the tractor," Papaw Merry said as he entered.

"Let's all get to the dining room. It's time to eat," Mom said before everyone got their conversations into high gear.

I never had to be told twice to get to the table, especially on a day like today. We pulled in a few extra chairs from the kitchen so that everyone could have a seat. It was crowded whenever everyone got seated, but it sure was special.

We squeezed together while Dad asked the blessing on the food. We bowed our heads and Dad prayed, "Dear Heavenly Father, we thank You for this gathering and everyone that is here. We thank You for the food and the nice warm home that You have given us. May the food be blessed and give us the strength that we need and may everything we do and say be pleasing to You. Forgive us of our sins. We ask this all in Jesus' name, Amen."

"Amens" resounded around the table, and we all dug in. I went straight to the sweet potato casserole. I loved the hard sugary topping. There never was enough room on my plate for what I actually wanted to pile on, so I put on what I could and hoped there would be enough left for seconds.

"My, oh my! Did you and the girls do all of this?" Papaw Merry complimented.

Mom, who was busy getting food for the twins, answered, "Gil and Hallie are really getting to be handy in the kitchen."

Papaw Grove continued the volley of words. "Don't teach 'em too much, or every bachelor in the county will be trying to marry them,"

One thing that was certain: My two Papaws sure could get a conversation going and keep it going.

The talking slowed considerably as everybody began to eat. Luckily there was enough turkey and dressing left for me to get a second helping. I left only a little room in my stomach for pumpkin pie. Before dessert was served, Papaw Grove and Papaw Merry started talking about the good ole days. They called each other by their last names only. I think that stemmed from their military days.

"Grove, do you remember when Arden and Erin first started courting?" Papaw Merry asked while wiping his mouth.

"Oh, yeah. How could I forget Arden and his three-legged, one-eyed, bobtailed dog?" Papaw Grove answered with a chuckle.

"Erin, you just loved that dog, didn't you?" Dad chimed in.

"How come someone brings that dog up at almost every decent meal we have around here?" Mom asked with a puzzled expression.

"I guess it's because Friday became sort of a novelty in the community and everyone knew about all of his calamities," Papaw Grove replied.

"I'd really like to change the subject," Mom suggested.

"What on earth is better to talk about than Friday?" Papaw Merry inquired.

I had to jump into the conversation. "Dad! Before you change the subject, can you tell us what finally happened to Friday?" I asked.

"We've heard how he lost his leg, eye, and tail, but you've never told us what happened to him after that."

"You mean he's never told you what happened to Friday?" both Papaws asked simultaneously.

A very strong "NO" rang out from all of us kids.

Dad put down his napkin, leaned back in his chair, and told us the rest of the story about his three-legged, one-eyed, bobtailed dog, Friday.

"To begin, you gotta remember that Friday had lost some of his senses and much of his physical identity. Despite his numerous handicaps, he still hunted like a fool. There wasn't a day that passed that Friday didn't attempt to run down a cottontail. One thing Friday was notorious for was trying to get to a rabbit even after it went into the hole. There had been times when I'd have to pull Friday out of a hole.

"Well, it was a cool fall morning, and Friday had been running a rabbit since dawn. His bark echoed in the holler, and after about two hours, the barking stopped. I never thought anything of it. Rabbits go in the hole all of the time. As I went outside to get some firewood, I looked up and saw Friday's hind leg and nubby tail sticking straight up out of a rabbit hole. I dropped my armload of wood and went to rescue my determined dog. When I grabbed his leg I noticed that Friday felt sort of strange. I gave only a slight pull and when Friday popped out of the hole, a cottontail twice the normal size shot out of the hole.

"Friday didn't pursue the rabbit because he had died. He hadn't smothered, because he wasn't really lodged in the hole at all. To this day I think that gigantic rabbit scared my dog to death. He was quite old."

I was a bit shocked by the story's ending but not all stories end with happily ever after.

The remainder of the day was nothing short of a real blessing. After eating we shared gifts, and the neatest thing was that our grandparents Grove and our grandparents Merry went in together and bought each of us a Holy Bible with our name on the front. No gift ever meant so much.

By the end of the evening, all of our grandparents had left and all was quiet in the house. I lay under the Christmas tree looking up through the branches at the colorful lights. My heart was happy that we had such a great day, but it was sad that yet another Christmas had passed. I lay there and was thankful, but most of all, I lay there and hoped for yet another Merry Christmas.

40

Looking Back

As soon as Christmas was over, I always got this strange feeling that I needed to stop and look back at the year gone by. Maybe it was the farmer in me that made me think that way. You see, farmers were always looking back on the season in order to learn from both their accomplishments and mistakes.

The year had certainly been eventful. I had passed the sixth grade and moved on to be a poet laureate in Miss Frances' class. Thankfully, Orin had moved on to the high school where Gil and Hallie could keep an eye on him. And who could forget that Orin and I found the biggest ginseng root ever and were "Ginseng Heroes" for a while.

Let's not forget that Orin whacked me in the leg with a weedeater and Billy Whittle married Miss Bass. Boy, now that was a day. The burley season had gone great, and we had a record sale at the market.

Of course, I can't neglect to mention that I made a new best friend, Ian Best. Oh, how I hoped his Christmas was merry. And to top things off, Mom bought Dad a bigger tractor for Christmas. Wow! What an eventful year it had been!

God had been so good to us throughout yet another year.

41

Looking Forward

The season of Christmas had passed, but the meaning would burn on throughout the entire year. The days that followed our family dinner were cold and restful. Even Dad caught up on some much needed rest.

I got up early on December 31 just to ponder a bit more.

Now that we were standing on the threshold of a new year, I also liked to look forward to what may lie ahead. When I think of the words that so many people will hear at 12:00 a.m. on January the first, "Happy New Year!" I can't help but wonder what kind of happiness may be in store for our family.

I stood with my face pressed up against the window, the same place I was standing when we began this story, and I looked out over the fields and the pastures that had been graced with a heavy frost. The cattle were standing in a large huddle and I could see their breath rising in the cold air. It was hard to believe that the season was gone and, most of all, another year was about to pass us by.

No doubt, a lot would change in the year to come. We knew that we'd possibly have to bale our tobacco instead of hand tying. Now that we had a bigger tractor, who knows, Dad may take on more leases and farm more burley. Time could only tell about those things, but there was one thing for certain: No matter what, there would certainly be many more family field days to come.

Jarrod E. Stephens, with one of his favorite legacies—
the Stephens' family tractor, a 1972 Massey Ferguson 135.

About the Author

Jarrod E. Stephens is an elementary teacher with a B.A. and Masters degree in Middle Grades Education. Jarrod is a youth leader at his home church, Emmanuel Missionary Baptist Church, located in Eastern, Kentucky, where he, his wife, and sons attend. His years of teaching and working with youth have given him a passion for writing original works that will embolden God's children and teach them simple truths of His Word.

Having grown up on a small family farm in Eastern Kentucky, Jarrod's firsthand knowledge of the rural way of life will give readers a factual account of the way life was and still is for many families living there. Jarrod still farms and hopes that his sons will continue tilling the soil just as their family has done for so many years. In fact, the tractor pictured on the cover, and to the left of this page, is indeed the Stephens' family tractor: a 1972 Massey Ferguson 135. "I learned nearly everything I know about farming while sitting atop it," Jarrod says. "My plans are to restore it someday and to let my sons learn to farm on the same tractor I did.

"*Family Field Days* was born from my love for the simple farming life. Growing up on a tobacco farm in Eastern Kentucky, I witnessed firsthand the bonds and friendships that were created in communities and families. Families worked together in the fields to make ends meet and through the many trials they faced together, they grew stronger. As the government began a buyout program, many smalltime farmers sold their burley tobacco quotas and a culture that had existed for so long began to die away. Now, many of the fields are overgrown and tobacco barns stand in disrepair. As I witnessed the culture change and in some aspects go away completely, I felt compelled to attempt to preserve the beauty of life in rural Kentucky in my own words."

You may email Jarrod at: **familyfielddays@gmail.com**

LaVergne, TN USA
06 July 2010
188482LV00001B/185/P